A Single Shard

Linda Sue Park

ROCK THE BOAT

To Dinah,
because she asked for another book.

A Rock the Boat Book

This edition first published in Great Britain by Rock the Boat,
an imprint of Oneworld Publications, 2022

Text copyright © Linda Sue Park, 2001, 2022

The moral right of Linda Sue Park to be identified as the Author of this
work has been asserted by her in accordance with the Copyright, Designs
and Patents Act 1988

ISBN 978-0-86154-186-7
eISBN 978-0-86154-187-4

Printed and bound in Great Britain by Clays Ltd, Elcograf S.p.A.

This book is a work of fiction. Names, characters, businesses, organisa-
tions, places and events are either the product of the author's imagination
or are used fictitiously. Any resemblance to actual persons, living or dead,
events, or locales is entirely coincidental.

Oneworld Publications
10 Bloomsbury Street
London WC1B 3SR
England

MIX
Paper from
responsible sources
FSC® C018072
www.fsc.org

To UK readers, on the twentieth-anniversary edition of *A Single Shard*

Pottery in twelfth-century Korea? Not a typical subject for a children's book. I've been asked many times how I came to write *A Single Shard*, and the short answer is: because of reading. Here's a much longer answer.

Once upon a time, there was a young Korean couple. They had emigrated to the United States only a few years earlier, and they were still learning to speak English. They were living outside Chicago, and a city newspaper ran on its pages a single-frame cartoon that taught the alphabet phonetically. The young woman cut out every one of those cartoons and glued them onto the pages of one of her old college textbooks. In this way, she made an alphabet book for her four-year-old daughter. And so it was that on her first day of school, that little girl, the daughter of Korean immigrants, was the only child in her reception class who could already read.

That was how my life as a reader began—like so many stories, with a mother. Mine continues with a father who took me to the library. *He took me to the library.* Every three weeks without fail, unless we were out of town, he spent an hour on Saturday morning choosing books for my siblings and me.

A few years ago, I was thinking about how my father must have known very little about English-language children's literature when we were growing up. So I asked him, 'How did you choose books for us?' 'Oh—I'll show you,' he said. He left the room for a few moments and came back with a battered accordion file and handed it to me. Inside were dozens of publications listing recommended children's books—brochures, flyers, pamphlets. I owe most of my childhood reading to the fact that librarians love to make lists!

The importance of my library upbringing was brought home to me in an unexpected way with the publication of my first book, *Seesaw Girl*. In the summer of 1999, my editor Dinah Stevenson sent me my first author copy, and as you might imagine, it was one of the most thrilling moments of my life. It was unquestionably the most beautiful book that had ever been published. But…but…something was bothering me. Something about it wasn't quite right, and I couldn't figure out what it was.

A few weeks later, I had my first book signing. A woman with a book bag approached the table and said, 'I'm a librarian. I already bought two copies of your book for our collection—would you mind signing previously purchased copies?' Of course I didn't mind, so she pulled the two books out of her bag and handed them to me.

They were already covered with that clear cellophane—you know the stuff I mean. And it was like a lightning bolt—THAT was what had been missing from my first author copy! That transparent cover was what made a 'real' book!

If it weren't for libraries, I don't think I would have become a writer.

In my reading about Korea, I came across the information that in the eleventh and twelfth centuries, Korea had produced the finest pottery in the world, better than even China's. I was excited to learn about this exquisite pottery, and I wanted to share what I had learned.

The ending of the book came to me in a single moment: in a book about Korean art, I saw a photograph of a beautiful celadon vase covered with cranes and clouds. I knew in that instant that the character in the book would grow up to make that vase. And for him to make such a remarkable work of art, he would need not only tremendous craftsmanship, but also a great love for someone who had something to do with cranes.

Much later, after the book was finished, I realized that the story owed a huge debt to another book: *I, Juan de Pareja,* by Elizabeth Borton de Treviño (which won the Newbery Medal in 1966). In that book, the orphaned black slave Juan de Pareja becomes an assistant to the famed painter Velázquez and is eventually freed by his master, which enables him to pursue his own painting career. The ending speculates on how a certain Velázquez work came to be painted, just as *A Single Shard* speculates about that vase.

It's impossible for me to write without discovering connections to reading. I often feel as if every writer whose work I've loved is mentoring me.

Connections. Making connections has always been the most important element of story to me. Connections to another time and place, and to my own ethnic background in historical fiction; connections to a character within the text; connections to people around us because of a text.

During my son's teenage years, we didn't get along very well. I knew it was normal adolescent/parent stuff, but that did not make it any easier. I would like to quote from an email that I sent to another author after my son and I had finally gotten through that difficult time:

'…It seems I have only one good memory of our relationship during that eternal year: your books. We talked about daemons endlessly, assigning them to each other, everyone we knew, television personalities, strangers, and so on…We consoled each other when we lost Lee Scoresby. In a hundred ways the books gave us things to talk about during a time when it seemed any other attempt at communication was doomed to end in raised voices and slammed doors.

…I admire many things about the series and about your other books too. But it is one thing to admire certain books, and another to say they have truly made a difference in a person's life. Thank you most sincerely for the difference His Dark Materials has made in mine.'

Many of you will have recognized that the author is Philip Pullman. In another email to a literature group, he ended his message with the exhortation to 'Include! Include!' When I read that, my idea of the importance of 'connection' was at once broadened. As well as connections—those straight lines of contact—inclusion seems equally apt, the idea of widening the circle: widening the audience for books about all sorts of places and times and people.

To 'include' also means to widen the experience of young readers by giving them books they might not have chosen for themselves, in the hope that they will find their own connections within the pages. I would like to express my sincere gratitude to the teachers, librarians, educators, booksellers, and other adults who have taken on this task, for which every reader and writer in the world should be grateful. My thanks also to Rock the Boat for bringing out this lovely twentieth-anniversary edition of *A Single Shard.*

When I was a child in the 1960s, it seemed like very few people in the US or Europe knew about Korea. People would ask me, 'Are you Chinese or Japanese?' (This was long before the current era of Samsung and BTS and K-drama.) I grew up feeling that there was nothing noteworthy about being Korean.

I could not have been more wrong. What I know now is that *everyone* has stories that are worth sharing. Every family, every community, every culture. That means you and your family. You don't have to be a writer, if that's not your thing: you can make music or videos or podcasts; you can dance or draw or become an activist—there are endless ways to share stories. It's vital that we all find a way that works for us, because sharing stories makes the world a better place: injustice happens when not enough of us share our stories and when those stories are not shared enough.

From Korean mythology comes this definition of an eon: the length of time it takes for a heavenly spirit to wear a mountain down to a pebble—by stroking it with a feather. All of us are here in this world for only a single stroke of that feather, but together we can wear away the most intractable rock of a problem. And we can make our time count even more by touching the lives of others—especially the young people who follow us. So. . .

Connect! Include!

A small village on the west coast of Korea,
mid- to late 12th century

CHAPTER

1

'Eh, Tree-ear! Have you hungered well today?' Crane-man called out as Tree-ear drew near the bridge.

The well-fed of the village greeted each other politely by saying, 'Have you eaten well today?' Tree-ear and his friend turned the greeting inside out for their own little joke.

Tree-ear squeezed the bulging pouch that he wore at his waist. He had meant to hold back the good news, but the excitement spilled out of him. 'Crane-man! A good thing that you greeted me so just now, for later today we will have to use the proper words!' He held the bag high. Tree-ear was delighted when Crane-man's eyes widened in surprise. He knew that Crane-man would guess at once—only one thing could give a bag that kind of smooth fullness. Not turnip-tops or chicken bones, which protruded in odd lumps. No, the bag was filled with *rice*.

1

Crane-man raised his walking crutch in a salute. 'Come, my young friend! Tell me how you came by such a fortune—a tale worth hearing, no doubt!'

Tree-ear had been trotting along the road on his early-morning perusal of the village rubbish heaps. Ahead of him a man carried a heavy load on a *jiggeh*, an open-framed backpack made of branches. On the *jiggeh* was a large woven-straw container, the kind commonly used to carry rice.

Tree-ear knew that the rice must be from last year's crop; in the fields surrounding the village this season's rice had only just begun to grow. It would be many months before the rice was harvested and the poor allowed to glean the fallen grain from the bare fields. Only then would they taste the pure flavour of rice and feel its solid goodness in their bellies. Just looking at the straw box made water rush into Tree-ear's mouth.

The man had paused in the road and hoisted the wooden *jiggeh* higher on his back, shifting the cumbersome weight. As Tree-ear stared, rice began to trickle out of a hole in the straw box. The trickle thickened and became a stream. Oblivious, the man continued on his way.

For a few short moments Tree-ear's thoughts wrestled with one another. *Tell him—quickly! Before he loses too much rice!*

No! Don't say anything—you will be able to pick up the fallen rice after he rounds the bend . . .

Tree-ear made his decision. He waited until the man had reached the bend in the road, then ran to catch him.

'Honourable sir,' Tree-ear said, panting and bowing. 'As I walked behind you, I noticed that you are marking your path with rice!'

The farmer turned and saw the trail of rice. A well-built man with a broad suntanned face, he pushed his straw hat back, scratched his head, and laughed ruefully.

'Impatience,' said the farmer. 'I should have had this container woven with a double wall. But it would have taken more time. Now I pay for not waiting a bit longer.' He struggled out of the *jiggeh*'s straps and inspected the container. He prodded the straw to close the gap but to no avail, so he threw his arms up in mock despair. Tree-ear grinned. He liked the farmer's easygoing nature.

'Fetch me a few leaves, boy,' said the farmer. Tree-ear complied, and the man stuffed them into the container as a temporary patch.

The farmer squatted to don the *jiggeh*. As he started walking, he called over his shoulder. 'Good deserves good, urchin. The rice on the ground is yours if you can be troubled to gather it.'

'Many thanks, kind sir!' Tree-ear bowed, very pleased

with himself. He had made a lucky guess, and his waist pouch would soon be filled with rice.

Tree-ear had learned from Crane-man's example. Foraging in the woods and rubbish heaps, gathering fallen grain-heads in the autumn—these were honourable ways to garner a meal, requiring time and work. But stealing and begging, Crane-man said, made a man no better than a dog.

'Work gives a man dignity, stealing takes it away,' he often said.

Following Crane-man's advice was not always easy for Tree-ear. Today, for example. Was it stealing, to wait as Tree-ear had for more rice to fall before alerting the man that his rice bag was leaking? Did a good deed balance a bad one? Tree-ear often pondered these kinds of questions, alone or in discussion with Crane-man.

'Such questions serve in two ways,' Crane-man had explained. 'They keep a man's mind sharp—and his thoughts off his empty stomach.'

Now, as always, he seemed to know Tree-ear's thoughts without hearing them spoken. 'Tell me about this farmer,' he said. 'What kind of man was he?'

Tree-ear considered the question for several moments, stirring his memory. At last, he answered, 'One who lacks patience—he said it himself. He had not wanted to wait for a sturdier container to be built. And he could not be bothered to pick up the fallen rice.' Tree-ear paused. 'But he laughed easily, even at himself.'

'If he were here now, and heard you tell of waiting a little longer before speaking, what do you think he would say or do?'

'He would laugh,' Tree-ear said, surprising himself with the speed of his response. Then, more slowly, 'I think . . . he would not have minded.'

Crane-man nodded, satisfied. And Tree-ear thought of something his friend often said: *Scholars read the great words of the world. But you and I must learn to read the world itself.*

Tree-ear was so called after the mushroom that grew in wrinkled half-circles on dead or fallen tree trunks, emerging from the rotten wood without benefit of parent seed. A good name for an orphan, Crane-man said. If ever Tree-ear had had another name, he no longer remembered it, nor the family that might have named him so.

Tree-ear shared the space under the bridge with Crane-man—or rather, Crane-man shared it with him. After all, Crane-man had been there first, and would not be leaving anytime soon. The shrivelled and twisted calf and foot he had been born with made sure of that.

Tree-ear knew the story of his friend's name. 'When they saw my leg at birth, it was thought I would not survive,' Crane-man had said. 'Then, as I went through life on one leg, it was said that I was like a crane. But besides standing on one leg, cranes are also a symbol of long life.' True enough, Crane-man added. He had outlived all his family and, unable to work, had been forced to sell his possessions one by one, including, at last, the roof over his head. Thus it was that he had come to live under the bridge.

Once, a year or so earlier, Tree-ear had asked him how long he had lived there. Crane-man shook his head; he no longer remembered. But then he brightened and hobbled over to one side of the bridge, beckoning Tree-ear to join him.

'I do not remember how long I have been here,' he said, 'but I know how long *you* have.' And he pointed upwards, to the underside of the bridge. 'I wonder that I have not shown you this before.'

On one of the slats was a series of deep scratches, as if made with a pointed stone. Tree-ear examined them, then shook his head at Crane-man. 'So?'

'One mark for each spring since you came here,' Crane-man explained. 'I kept count of your years, for I thought the time would come when you would like to know how old you are.'

Tree-ear looked again, this time with keen interest. There was a mark for each finger of both hands—ten marks in all.

Crane-man answered before Tree-ear asked. 'No, you have more than ten years,' he said. 'When you first came and I began making those marks, you were in perhaps your second year—already on two legs and able to talk.'

Tree-ear nodded. He knew the rest of the story already. Crane-man had learned but little from the man who had brought Tree-ear to the bridge. The man had been paid by a kindly monk in the city of Songdo to bring Tree-ear to the little seaside village of Ch'ulp'o. Tree-ear's parents had died of fever, and the monk knew of an uncle in Ch'ulp'o.

When the travellers arrived, the man discovered that the uncle no longer lived there, the house having been abandoned long before. He took Tree-ear to the temple on the mountainside, but the monks had been unable to take the boy in because fever raged there as well. The villagers told the man to take the child to the bridge, where Crane-man would care for him until the temple was free of sickness.

'And,' Crane-man always said, 'when a monk came to fetch you a few months later, you would not leave. You clung to my good leg like a monkey to a tree, not crying but not letting go, either! The monk went away. You stayed.'

When Tree-ear was younger, he had asked for the story often, as if hearing it over and over again might reveal something more—what his father's trade had been, what his mother had looked like, where his uncle had gone—but there was never anything more. It no longer mattered. If there was more to having a home than Crane-man and the bridge, Tree-ear had neither knowledge nor need of it.

Breakfast that morning was a feast—a bit of the rice boiled to a gruel in a cast-off earthenware pot, served up in a bowl carved from a gourd. And Crane-man produced yet another surprise to add to the meal: two chicken leg-bones. No flesh remained on the arid bones, but the two friends cracked them open and worried away every scrap of marrow from inside.

Afterwards, Tree-ear washed in the river and fetched a gourd of water for Crane-man, who never went into the river if he could help it; he hated getting his feet wet. Then Tree-ear set about tidying up the area under the bridge. He took care to keep the place neat, for he disliked having to clear a space to sleep at the tired end of the day.

Housekeeping complete, Tree-ear left his companion and set off back up the road. This time he did not zigzag between rubbish heaps but strode purposefully towards a small house set apart from the others at a curve in the road.

Tree-ear slowed as he neared the mud-and-wood struc-ture. He tilted his head, listening, and grinned when the droning syllables of a song-chant reached his ears. The master potter Min was singing, which meant that it was a 'throwing' day.

Min's house backed onto the beginnings of the foothills and their brushy growth, which gave way to pine-wooded mountains beyond. Tree-ear swung wide of the house. Under the deep eaves at the back, Min kept his potter's wheel. He was there now, his grey head bent over the wheel, chanting his wordless song.

Tree-ear made his way cautiously to his favourite spot, behind a paulownia tree whose low branches kept him hidden from view. He peeped through the leaves and caught his breath in delight. Min was just beginning a new pot.

Min threw a mass of clay the size of a cabbage onto the centre of the wheel. He picked it up and threw it again, threw it several times. After one last throw he sat down and stared at the clay for a moment. Using his foot to spin the base of the wheel, he placed dampened hands on the sluggardly lump, and for the hundredth time Tree-ear watched the miracle.

In only a few moments the clay rose and fell, grew taller, then rounded down, until it curved into perfect symmetry. The spinning slowed. The chant, too, died out and became a mutter of words that Tree-ear could not hear.

Min sat up straight. He crossed his arms and leaned back a little, as if to see the vase from a distance. Turning the wheel slowly with his knee, he inspected the graceful shape for invisible faults. Then, 'Pah!' He shook his head and in a single motion of disgust scooped up the clay and slapped it back onto the wheel, whereupon it collapsed into an oafish lump again, as if ashamed.

Tree-ear opened his mouth to let out his breath silently, only then realizing that he had been keeping it back. To his eyes the vase had been perfect, its width half its height, its curves like those of a flower petal. Why, he wondered, had Min found it unworthy? What had he seen that so displeased him?

Min never failed to reject his first attempt. Then he would repeat the whole process. This day Tree-ear was able to watch the clay rise and fall four times before Min was satisfied. Each of the four efforts had looked identical to Tree-ear, but something about the fourth pleased Min. He took a length of twine and slipped it deftly under the vase to release it from the wheel, then placed the vase carefully on a tray to dry.

As Tree-ear crept away, he counted the days on his fingers. He knew the potter's routine well; it would be many days before another throwing day.

The village of Ch'ulp'o faced the sea, its back to the mountains and the river edging it like a neat seam. Its potters produced the delicate celadon ware that had achieved fame not only in Korea but as far away as the court of the Chinese emperor.

Ch'ulp'o had become an important village for ceramics by virtue of both its location and its soil. On the shore of the Western Sea, it had access both to the easiest sea route northward and to plentiful trade with China. And the clay from the village pits contained exactly the right amount of iron to produce the exquisite grey-green colour of celadon so prized by collectors.

Tree-ear knew every potter in the village, but until recently he had known them only for their rubbish heaps. It was hard for him to believe that he had never taken the time to watch them at work before. In recent years the pottery from the village kilns had gained great favour among those wealthy enough to buy pieces as gifts for both the royal court and the Buddhist temples, and the potters had achieved new levels of prosperity. The pickings from their rubbish heaps had become richer in consequence, and for the first time Tree-ear was able to forget about his stomach for a few hours each day.

During those hours it was Min he chose to watch most closely. The other potters kept their wheels in small windowless shacks. But in the warm months Min preferred to work beneath the eaves behind his house, open to the breeze and the view of the mountains.

Working without walls meant that Min possessed great skill and the confidence to match it. Potters guarded their secrets jealously. A new shape for a teapot, a new inscribed design—these were things that the potters refused to reveal until a piece was ready to show to a buyer.

Min did not seem to care about such secrecy. It was as if he were saying, *Go ahead, watch me. No matter—you will not be able to imitate my skill.*

It was true, and it was also the main reason that Tree-ear loved watching Min. His work was the finest in the region, perhaps even in the whole country.

CHAPTER

2

Tree-ear peered between the leaves of the paulownia tree, puzzled. Several days had passed since his last visit to Min's house, and he had calculated that it was time for another throwing day. But there was no sign of Min at his work, nor any wet clay on the wheel. The workshop area was tidy, with a few chickens in the yard the only signs of life.

Emboldened by the silence, Tree-ear emerged from his hiding place and approached the house. Against the wall was a set of shelves holding a few of Min's latest creations. They were at the stage the potters called 'leather-hard'—dried by the air but not yet glazed or fired. Unglazed, the work was of little interest to thieves. The finished pieces were surely locked up somewhere in the house.

13

Tree-ear paused at the edge of the brush and listened hard one last time. A hen clucked proudly, and Tree-ear grinned—Min would have an egg for his supper. But there was still no sign of the potter, so Tree-ear tiptoed the last few steps to stand before the shelves.

For the first time he was seeing Min's work at close range. There was a duck that would have fitted in the palm of his hand, with a tiny hole in its bill. Tree-ear had seen such a duck in use before. A painter had been sitting on the riverbank, working on a water scene. The painter had poured water from the duck's bill onto a stone a single drop at a time, mixing ink to exactly the correct consistency for his work.

Tree-ear stared at Min's duck. Though it was now a dull grey, so detailed were its features that he found himself half listening for the sound of a quack. Min had shaped and then carved the clay to form curve of wing and tilt of head. Even the little tail curled up with an impudence that made Tree-ear smile.

He tore his gaze away from the duck to examine the next piece, a tall jug with ribbed lines that imitated the shape of a melon. The lines were perfectly symmetrical, curving so gracefully from top to bottom that Tree-ear longed to run his finger along the smooth shallow grooves. The melon's stem and leaves were cleverly shaped to form the lid of the jug.

The last piece on the shelf was the least interesting—a rectangular lidded box as large as his two hands. It was completely undecorated. Disappointed in its plainness, Tree-ear was ready to turn away when a thought struck him. Outside, the box was plain, but perhaps inside . . .

Holding his breath, he reached out, gently lifted the lid, and looked inside. He grinned in double delight at his own correct guess and at Min's skill. The plain box held five smaller boxes—a small round one in the centre and four curved boxes that fitted around it perfectly. The small boxes appeared to completely fill the larger container, but Min had left exactly the right amount of space to allow any of them to be lifted out.

Tree-ear put the lid of the large box down on the shelf and picked up one of the curved containers. On the underside of its lid was a lip of clay that held the lid in place. Tree-ear's eyes flickered back and forth between the small pieces in his hand and the larger container, his brow furrowed in thought.

How did Min fit them together so perfectly? Perhaps he made the large box, then a second one to fit inside, and cut the smaller boxes from that? Or did he make an inside box first and fit the larger box around it? Maybe he began with the small central box, then the curved ones, then—

Someone shouted. The chickens squawked noisily and Tree-ear dropped what he was holding. He stood there, paralysed for a moment, then threw his hands up in front of his face to protect himself from the blows that were raining down on his head and shoulders.

It was the old potter. 'Thief!' he screamed. 'How dare you come here! How dare you touch my work!'

Tree-ear did the only thing he could think of. He dropped to his knees and cowered in a deep formal bow.

'Please! Please, honourable sir, I was not stealing your work—I came only to admire it.'

Min's cane halted in mid-blow. The potter stood over the boy with the cane still poised for another strike.

'Have you been here before, beggar-boy?'

Tree-ear's thoughts scrambled about as he tried to think what to answer. The truth seemed easiest.

'Yes, honourable sir. I come often to watch you work.'
'Ah!'

Tree-ear was still doubled over in his bow, but out of the corner of his eye, he could see the tip of the cane as it was lowered to the ground. He allowed himself a single sigh of relief.

'So is it you who breaks the twigs and bruises the leaves of the paulownia tree just beyond?'

Tree-ear nodded, feeling his face flush. He had thought he was covering his tracks well.

'Not to steal, you say? How do I know you do not watch just to see when I have made something of extra value?'

Now Tree-ear raised his head and looked at Min. He kept his voice respectful, but his words were proud.

'I would not steal. Stealing and begging make a man no better than a dog.'

The potter stared at the boy for a long moment. At last, Min seemed to make up his mind about something, and when he spoke again, his voice had lost the sharpest edge of its anger.

'So you were not stealing. It is the same thing to me—with one part damaged, the rest is of no use.' He gestured at the misshapen pottery box on the ground, badly dented from its fall. 'Get on your way, then. I know better than to ask for payment for what you have ruined.'

Tree-ear stood slowly, shame hot in his breast. It was true. He could never hope to pay Min for the damaged box.

Min picked it up and tossed it on the rubbish heap at the side of the yard. He continued to mutter crossly. 'Ai, three days' work, and for what? For nothing. I am behind now. The order will be late . . .'

Tree-ear had taken a few dragging steps out of the yard. But on hearing the old potter's mutterings, he lifted his head and turned back towards him.

'Honourable potter? Sir? Could I not work for you, as payment? Perhaps my help could save you some time . . .'

Min shook his head impatiently. 'What could you do, an untrained child? I have no time to teach you—you would be more trouble than help.'

Tree-ear stepped forward eagerly. 'You would not need to teach so much as you think, sir. I have been watching you for many months now. I know how you mix the clay, and turn the wheel—I have watched you make many things . . .'

The potter waved one hand to cut off the boy's words and spoke with derision. 'Turn the wheel! Ha! He thinks he can sit and make a pot—just like that!'

Tree-ear crossed his arms stubbornly and did not look away. Min picked up the rest of the box set and tossed it too on the rubbish heap. He muttered under his breath, so Tree-ear could not hear the words.

Min straightened up and glanced around, first at his shelf, then at the wheel, and finally at Tree-ear.

'Yes, all right,' he said, his voice still rough with annoyance. 'Come tomorrow at daybreak, then. Three days it took me to make that box, so you will give me nine days' work in return. I cannot even begin to think how much greater the value of my work is than yours, but we will settle on this for a start.'

Tree-ear bowed in agreement. He walked around the

side of the house, then flew off down the road. He could hardly wait to tell Crane-man. For the first time in his life he would have real work to do.

Upon arriving the next day for work, Tree-ear learned that it was Min's turn to chop wood for the kiln fires. That was why he had not been at home the day before.

Like most of the potters' villages, Ch'ulp'o had a communal kiln. Set on the hillside just outside the centre of the village, it looked like a long, low tunnel made of hardened clay. The potters took turns using the kiln and keeping up the supply of fuel.

Min handed Tree-ear a small axe and led him around the side of the house to a wheeled cart.

'Fill the cart with wood,' Min barked. 'Dry wood, not wet. Do not come back until the cart is full.'

Tree-ear felt as though the sun had suddenly dimmed. The night before, sleep had not come easily. He had imagined himself at the wheel, a beautiful pot growing from the clay before him. Perhaps, he thought now, if he chopped enough wood quickly, there would still be time at the end of the day . . .

Min quashed that hope with his next words. 'Take care to go well into the mountains,' he said. 'Far too many trees have been cut too close to the village. You will walk a long way before you find a plentiful stand of trees.'

Tree-ear swallowed a sigh as he placed the axe in the cart. Grasping the two handles, he wheeled the cart onto the road. He turned to wave farewell, but the potter was no longer there. The sound of the throwing song floated out from behind the house.

Chopping wood for hours without a single bite to eat had been hard enough. But the worst of that day was the long trip back down the mountainside with the cart full of wood.

The path was rutted and bumpy. The homemade cart was poorly balanced, awkward with its heavy load. At every step Tree-ear had to keep his eyes trained on the path and the cart. In spite of his efforts, whenever the wheels hit a deep rut, the cart tipped precariously and some of the logs spilled out. Then he had to stop to pick up the fallen wood. It was more than annoying, because he had been careful to lay the wood neatly as he chopped, and each bump led to further disarray of the tidy pile.

After this had happened more times than he could count, Tree-ear neared the end of the mountain path. Soon it would widen and smooth out into the more heavily travelled foothills road. Tree-ear lifted his head for a moment, in eager anticipation of the end of his journey.

Just then the right-hand wheel caught a stone. The cart handles were wrenched from his hands, and the cart tipped onto its side. The momentum pulled Tree-ear off balance, and he tripped over the cart and tumbled head-first to the ground.

He sat up, dazed. For a moment he didn't know whether to curse or cry. He set his lips together tightly and scrambled to his feet, then pulled the cart upright and began flinging the wood back into it in a frenzy.

As he heaved a large, rough log, an arrow of pain shot through his right hand. He cried out and clenched it into a fist for a moment until the throbbing eased a little. Then he opened it cautiously and examined the injury.

The pillow of fluid that had formed on his palm during the long hours of wielding the axe had burst. Blood ran from the wound, mixing with dirt and small bits of bark. Tree-ear stared at it, and he could not stop the tears that pressed hot behind his eyes.

Angrily, he blinked away the tears and set about tearing a strip of cloth from the bottom of his tunic. There was no water nearby, so he spat on his palm and wiped it as best he could, clenching his teeth against the pain. He used his other hand and his teeth to wrap and tie the cloth into a makeshift bandage.

From then on he worked slowly and methodically, stacking the wood in neat rows in the cart. The sun was low in the sky when he finished at last and wheeled the cart cautiously down the path to the foothills road.

Tree-ear dragged himself home to the bridge that evening. Crane-man's normally placid expression was replaced with a frown of worry when Tree-ear stumbled into the space under the struts and collapsed in a heap on the ground.

Crane-man said nothing. He merely held out a bowl in which he had placed a small mound of rice and a little pile of boiled greens. Too exhausted to eat, Tree-ear waved the food away. But Crane-man hobbled to his side and used his crutch for support as he eased himself down to sit next to Tree-ear. Crane-man picked up a little rice in his fingers, and insistently, but still without a word, began feeding Tree-ear as if he were a baby.

Tree-ear did not remember finishing the meal, but he awoke the next morning to see Crane-man swing himself down under the bridge by holding one of the struts, as he always did. Small and slight and who knew how old, Crane-man still moved his upper body with the ease of a young man; many were the times that Tree-ear forgot completely about the useless leg. Where had Crane-man been, so early?

Tree-ear sat up stiffly and began to rub his eyes. As he brought his right hand up to his face, he caught sight of the crude bandage. It was stiff with dried blood.

'Yes, that is what I have been about,' said Crane-man. 'Now, let us see what we can see.'

Tree-ear held out his hand. Crane-man untied the bandage and began to unwrap it.

'Sssst!' Tree-ear hissed sharply in pain and snatched his hand away. The final layer of cloth clung stubbornly to the wound, and Crane-man had been trying to pull it off.

'Come now, my monkey friend,' said Crane-man, kindly but firmly. 'It must be removed so we can clean the wound. The demons of sickness are no doubt already scheming to enter your body through such a door.'

Tree-ear rose and shuffled to the water's edge. He crouched and dipped his hand in the water. Its coolness soothed the throb, and its wetness loosened the cloth's grip on the wound. Wincing, he eased the bandage away.

While Tree-ear cleaned his wound, Crane-man took the strip of cloth and washed it thoroughly with water from the gourd bowl, scrubbing it against a flat stone at the river's edge. Then he wrung it out and handed it to Tree-ear, who scrambled up the bank and hung it on a strut to dry in the sun.

From his waist pouch Crane-man took a handful of green herbs he had gathered in the woods earlier that morning. He ground them to a paste between two stones, then scooped up some of the paste with two fingers and applied it to Tree-ear's hand.

'Close your hand,' Crane-man ordered. 'Squeeze, so the healing juices may enter the wound.'

The two friends ate the last of the rice-treasure for breakfast, Tree-ear holding the paste as he ate with his other hand. Then Crane-man tied the now-dry strip of cloth back into a bandage.

'There,' he said. 'A few days' rest will see that hand good as new.' He looked at Tree-ear sternly.

Tree-ear said nothing. He knew that Crane-man had already guessed there would be no rest that day. There was still eight days' work to be done for Min.

CHAPTER

3

Tree-ear trotted up the road toward Min's house. But he slowed a little when he heard the potter scolding him even before he arrived.

What kind of useless boy was he, coming back so late the day before and leaving the cart without a word? That wood should have been taken to the kiln and unloaded. Min had done it himself at dusk, and had nearly injured himself stumbling home in the darkness. Such help was worse than no help at all! Now, did Tree-ear really intend to make himself useful? If not, it would be better for him to forget their whole arrangement . . .

Finally, Min paused to draw breath. Tree-ear dared not look up. He felt like a beast with two heads, one ashamed, the other resentful. Ashamed that he had not finished the work properly, resentful that Min had not given him complete instructions. 'Fill the cart'—that had been the order, and he had done it. Was he expected to read Min's mind as well?

But the shame won out in Tree-ear. He feared being sent away before he could learn to make a pot.

'I am sorry that I displeased the honourable potter,' Tree-ear said. 'If he would be so good as to give me another chance, he will not be disappointed.'

'Hmph.' Min turned and walked towards the side of the house. Tree-ear stood still for a moment, unsure of what to do.

'Well?' Min turned back impatiently. 'Are you coming, beggar-boy, or are you a statue with your feet frozen to the ground?'

Tree-ear's joy at being forgiven was like a wisp of smoke; Min's orders for the day blew it into nothingness. His task was the same as the previous day's—to fill the cart with wood, and this time unload it at the kiln site.

Each day, Tree-ear appeared at Min's door eagerly. Each day, Min sent him up the mountain with the cart to chop more wood. At night, with Crane-man's careful ministrations, the wound on Tree-ear's hand would begin to heal, the tender pink layer toughening slightly. But at the start of the next day's work it would split and bleed again. Tree-ear came to expect the pain; the throbbing was like an unwelcome companion who appeared daily after the first few strokes of the axe.

On the third day, Crane-man had offered to come with him. Tree-ear's mind raced to think of a polite refusal. He knew what would happen: Crane-man would want to spare Tree-ear's blistered hand and would take up the axe himself. Tree-ear shuddered, picturing Crane-man trying to chop wood while leaning on his crutch. He might well injure his good leg.

'Your offer of help is kindness itself,' Tree-ear answered. 'But if it is all the same to you, it is far better for me to return to a meal already prepared. I could not imagine greater assistance than this.'

Crane-man was satisfied. It seemed to Tree-ear that his friend spent the entire day figuring out how to transform a handful of weeds and bones into something that resembled a meal.

Over the days Tree-ear developed a routine of work and rest. A period of diligent chopping and loading, then a break; this was better than several hours of frenzied chopping that left him with a vast, untidy pile of wood, which took much time to load and left him exhausted.

In the brief periods of rest he was sometimes able to gather a little food—a few wild mushrooms here, a handful of fern sprouts there. Crane-man had taught him well on their many walks through these mountains together. Tree-ear knew which mushrooms were tasty and which deadly. He knew the birds by their songs, and how a mountain lion's spoor looked different from that of a deer. And he never lost his way, for he knew where the streams ran, pointing sure as an arrow back down the mountain towards the road.

Besides his quiet times reading the mountain, Tree-ear's favourite part of the day was unloading the wood at the kiln site. The kiln was located at the far end of the village from Min's house. Nearby was a large, roughly built shed. Tree-ear wheeled the cart to the shed's entry, then carried armfuls of wood inside, where it would stay dry. The wood was stacked as high as a man could reach, in orderly piles on either side of a central aisle. Tree-ear liked arranging his wood neatly so the potters could take what they needed without the whole of the stack collapsing.

At the kiln site he often saw potters whose turn it was to use the kiln. They would greet him with a nod when he arrived. On the fourth day one of them spoke to him. 'You are Min's new boy, are you not?'

Tree-ear knew the potter who spoke; his name was Kang. He was old enough for grey to streak his hair, but younger than Min, with a keen eye and a restless manner. Tree-ear lowered the handles of the cart to the ground and bowed his head.

'High time the old man got himself some help.' Kang

spoke with what seemed like an edge to his voice. 'The last few times he did not bring anywhere near his proper share of wood.'

Then Kang stepped forward and began to help unload the cart, so Tree-ear's work was finished earlier than usual. He was left with time enough to rifle through a rubbish dump on his way home; the cabbage core that he found would add to Crane-man's culinary efforts for dinner.

It was the morning of the tenth day. The evening before, Tree-ear had returned the cart to its usual spot next to Min's house and had lingered about for a few moments. But Min did not emerge from the house, so Tree-ear had departed at last, his debt of work paid in full.

Awake for most of the night, Tree-ear had considered over and over how best to approach Min. In the nine days of work, Tree-ear had not once touched clay. He would never be able to make a pot unless he could continue his relationship with the potter.

Tree-ear rehearsed his words one last time as he neared Min's house. He drew in a breath and held it for a moment to steady himself, then called out, 'Master Potter?'

To Tree-ear's surprise, Min's wife opened the door. He knew, of course, that Min was married. On the days that he had spied on Min, Tree-ear had occasionally glimpsed the wife coming out to the yard to scatter grain for the chickens or to fetch water. But because she had nothing to do with the pottery work, Tree-ear had ignored her. And in the past several days of woodcutting he had not seen or thought of her at all.

Now he bowed his head as he stood before her. 'Is the master home?' he asked.

'He is at his breakfast,' she answered. 'You may wait at the back of the house.'

Tree-ear nodded his thanks and stepped away, but the woman spoke again, quietly. 'A good thing, your chopping the wood. He is not as young as he once was . . .' Her voice trailed off.

Tree-ear glanced up at her, and their eyes met. Hers were bright and soft, set in a small face netted with fine wrinkles. He dropped his gaze at once, not wishing to be considered impolite. *Like Crane-man's eyes*, he thought, and wondered why.

Min was washing his hands in a basin under the eaves when Tree-ear reached the back yard.

'What are you doing here?' Min's voice was cross, and he did not look up. 'It has been nine days and your debt is discharged. If you came to hear me say it, you can go now.'

Tree-ear bowed. 'I beg the honourable potter to pardon

my insolence,' he said. 'I wish to express my gratitude—'

'Yes, yes,' Min said impatiently. 'What is it?'

'It would be a great honour for me to continue working
for the potter.' Tree-ear began the speech he had planned
so carefully. 'If he would consider—'

'I cannot pay you.' Min's interruption could hardly
have been more abrupt, but the curt words swept over
Tree-ear like cool rain over a parched field. *I cannot pay
you* was the same as 'Yes'. A surge of joy lifted Tree-ear's
heart into his throat, so that he had to cough politely
before speaking again.

'To work for such a master is payment enough,' he
murmured.

'Temple bell until sundown, every day,' said Min.

Tree-ear found himself on the ground, collapsed in a
full bow of gratitude. It was all he could do to keep
himself from running all the way back to the bridge to
tell Crane-man the good news.

'Clay today, not wood.' Those were Min's orders for the
tenth day.

Once again Tree-ear trundled the cart, this time along
the river road, until he reached the digging area. Here the
clay had been cut away in neat slabs, leaving a pattern of
staggered rectangles in the riverbank.

Tree-ear paused for a moment when he reached the clay pits. He had passed by the pits many times before and had always liked looking at the scene there; the geometric pattern of the clay bank pleased him. But today he felt as though he were seeing the men and boys working there for the first time.

Using spades, they slashed at the clay with movements almost too swift to follow. When a slab of clay had been outlined with the spade, it was cut away from the bank and heaved into a nearby cart or basket.

Tree-ear watched for a while, the spade Min had given him on his shoulder. Then he slid down the muddy bank to stand in the shallow water. Raising the spade high over his shoulder, he brought it down with a dull *thunk*. It sliced into the wet clay, and Tree-ear noted with satisfaction the clean line made by the spade's edge. He tugged at the spade's handle, ready to make his next cut.

The spade did not budge. Tree-ear frowned, and pulled again. The head of the spade was well and truly buried. Tree-ear tried using both hands down low on the handle. The clay made squelching, sucking noises, as if it were trying to swallow the spade.

Finally, Tree-ear was forced to claw away the clay around the spade head in order to free it. His arms and legs were already covered with mud. He paused to brush away a mosquito and rubbed a swash of mud across one side of his face. At last, he stood up and swung the spade again.

It took him all morning to fill the cart with clay. The other diggers were long gone, having cut their clay with a swift skill that left Tree-ear alone and in despair. Heavy! The wet clay was far heavier than he had ever imagined. He could not begin to lift a slab with the spade; he had to cut each slab into several pieces and lift them one at a time into the cart. Tree-ear scowled to see the misshapen masses of clay in his cart, so different from the neat rectangles of the other workers.

Moreover, the spadework had torn open his blistered hand again. But it was not so painful as it had been on the mountainside, for here he could apply handfuls of cooling, soothing mud to the wound.

By the time the cart was loaded, Tree-ear wore mud like a second skin. Even raising his eyebrows was difficult, for his forehead was stiff with dried clay. And he was so exhausted that he could hardly bear the thought of wheeling the now-heavy cart back to Min's house.

Then a sudden thought came to him—dinner! He had forgotten in the toil of the morning. Apprentices, assistants, the lowliest workers in every trade—no matter what their status, it was the master's duty to provide a meal for them in the middle of the workday. Now that Tree-ear was no longer working off a debt, Min was obliged to feed him. The thought broke through Tree-ear's fatigue like a shaft of sunlight piercing a cloud.

He left the cart on the road and bounded into the river. He scrubbed and splashed and ducked under the water completely to get rid of as much grime as he possibly could. It would never do to appear for his first working meal dressed in mud.

Min glanced briefly at the clay-filled cart. 'You were long enough in returning,' he said with a sniff. 'I will not be able to do any more work until after my midday meal.'

He walked into the house, having said nothing about Tree-ear's food. But Tree-ear barely had time to wonder before Min's wife appeared in the doorway. She held out a parcel tied up in cloth.

Tree-ear trotted to the door, resisting the impulse to snatch the parcel from her. He bowed his head and held out his hands, palms up and together, as was proper when accepting something.

Min's wife placed the cloth package in his hands. 'Eat well, work well,' she said.

A hot lump rose in Tree-ear's throat. He raised his head and saw in her eyes that she heard his thanks even though he could not speak the words.

Tree-ear sat on a stone under the paulownia tree and untied the corners of the cloth. It held a gourd bowl filled with rice, whose whiteness was accented by a few dark shreds of savoury dried fish and a little pile of *kimchee*—pickled cabbage vivid with seasonings of red pepper, green onions, and garlic. A pair of chopsticks was laid neatly across the top of the bowl.

Tree-ear picked up the chopsticks and stared for a moment. Of one thing he was certain: the feast-day banquets in the palace of the king could never better the modest meal before him, for he had earned it.

Tree-ear carted another load of clay for Min that afternoon, then returned to the bridge where Crane-man had stewed some wild mushrooms for their supper. Tree-ear spoke eagerly about his work that day. It was not until Crane-man rose to gather the supper bowls that Tree-ear noticed something was missing.

The crutch. Sure enough, after handing Tree-ear the bowls to wash, Crane-man sat down with his knife and a sturdy straight branch and began to whittle a new crutch. Tree-ear wiped out the bowls, stacked them neatly on their rock shelf, and finally asked, 'What happened to the old one?'

Crane-man paused in his work, then waved his knife impatiently. 'Stupidity happened,' he answered. 'There was a run of flounder today.'

That was all he said, but Tree-ear heard much more.

Although Ch'ulp'o was on the sea, it was a potters' village, not a fishing village. The men and boys seldom took time from their work to fish. Still, they all knew the useful skill of fishing, and the women and girls often gathered shell-fish at low tide.

A run of flounder meant that a school of the tasty fish had come into shore far closer than usual; the waves even tossed fish right up on the beach. Such news sent many scrambling for their bamboo poles. But one had to be among the first to run from the village down to the shore. The flounder found their way back out to sea soon enough, and the fish flopping about on the sand were scooped up only by the quickest.

It had always been Tree-ear who skipped out to the beach at the first word of a flounder run, and he had never returned without a fat fish or two for a rare feast. Now he knew without asking that Crane-man had hobbled down to the beach and lurched about on the sand, so treacherous to his crutch, only to come away empty-handed.

Crane-man shaved another curl of wood, then held the crutch up to his eye, squinting to check that its lines were true. 'I was angry about not getting any fish,' he said as he returned to his whittling, 'so I struck my crutch against a rock. It broke, of course.'

A little pile of shavings had grown at Crane-man's feet.

Tree-ear crouched and stirred the pile with his finger, too ashamed to look up. In his mind he saw Crane-man making his slow, painful way back from the beach, with only a broken crutch to help him. And no fish for his trouble. How was it that in enjoying his noontime meal Tree-ear had forgotten his friend? He should have saved some of the food for Crane-man. If it had been the other way around, Crane-man would never have forgotten.

Tree-ear swept the shavings into his palm, then threw them into the river. As he watched the current carry them away, he mumbled, 'I am sorry about the flounder.'

'Ah, friend,' Crane-man said. 'You must mean, "I am sorry about your leg." Because that is the reason for our fishless supper today. But I think it a waste for either of us to spend too much time in sorrow over something we cannot change.' Crane-man grunted as he stood, then leaned on the new crutch to test it.

Satisfied, he nodded at Tree-ear. 'Besides, when I leave this world, I will have two good legs and no need for such as this.' And he tapped the crutch with his free hand.

Still cross with himself, Tree-ear grumbled half under his breath, 'Some of us will have *four* good legs.'

Crane-man batted at him with the new crutch. 'What are you saying, impudent boy? That I will be a beast in the next life?'

Tree-ear began to protest. 'No, not you—' Then he stopped and grinned. 'Well, maybe,' he said, putting his hand on his chin in an attitude of deep thought. 'A rabbit, I think. Very clever and quick—'

'You had better be quick now yourself!' Crane-man bellowed in mock anger, brandishing the crutch sword-fashion. Tree-ear began hopping about their little den like a rabbit, dodging Crane-man's jabs and swipes, his shame forgotten for the moment, as the day ended in laughter.

CHAPTER
4

In the morning Tree-ear presented himself at Min's door before the temple bell rang. As he had hoped, it was Min's wife who answered his call.

He held out a gourd bowl and bowed his head.

'I have brought my own bowl today, so as not to inconvenience the honourable potter's wife,' he said. Tree-ear's plan was to eat only half his food, leave the bowl hidden somewhere, and take the other half home to Crane-man at the end of the day.

Min's wife nodded and took the bowl from him, but he could see the puzzled look in her eyes. The day before, he had returned the bowl and chopsticks to her after washing and wiping them; clearly, there had been no need for him to bring his own bowl.

Tree-ear turned away, feeling guilt like a shadow across

his brow, and hoped fervently that he had not offended her. *I'm not really deceiving anyone*, he argued to himself. *And I haven't asked for more food—it should make no difference to her which bowl . . .*

He carted clay again for Min, and by mid-afternoon he had grown more accustomed to the work. He was learning the tricky balance of spadework—deep enough to make a clean cut, but not so deep as to bury the spade head in the mire. The work went more quickly now, and the muscles in his back and arms that had been strengthened by the woodcutting did not cry out so loudly any more.

Tree-ear brought the final load of clay back to Min's. As usual, the potter was nowhere in sight at the end of the day, so Tree-ear left the cart parked under the eaves and went to retrieve the remaining half of his midday meal.

Tree-ear caught his breath. The gourd bowl was not beneath the paulownia tree where he had left it. He searched the area around the tree. The bowl had been covered with a cloth weighed down by stones. Here was the cloth, snagged on a shrub—and there, a few paces further into the brush, the bowl.

Empty. Not just empty, but polished clean. Some wild animal . . .

Disappointment rose inside Tree-ear until he felt he

would have to let it escape in a wolf-like howl. Instead, he picked up the bowl and hurled it as far as he could into the brush.

'*Ai!*' The startled cry that came from somewhere within the overgrown brush frightened Tree-ear half off his feet. Min's wife emerged from behind a tangled bush, holding the bowl in one hand and a basket in the other. The basket was filled with berries, which she had apparently been gathering on the mountainside.

She was smiling gently as she handed him the bowl. 'This bowl had a great desire to become my hat,' she said. 'A bowl that flies! Small wonder that you preferred it to my own.' Tree-ear could see that she was teasing, but he was too deep in his own embarrassment and disappointment to respond with more than a curt nod. He checked himself in time to turn the nod into a bow of respect, then fled, leaving the scene of his failure but not the knowledge of it.

Yet again he had failed to share his meal with Crane-man. And on top of that, it seemed that he had nearly hit his master's wife on the head with his bowl.

It was two full moons now that Tree-ear had been working for Min, but it seemed like a year or even longer. He sometimes felt that he could hardly remember what his life had been like before. The days had acquired a rhythm, a regularity he found comforting and dependable. He woke early, worked for Min, ate half of his dinner, worked again, then returned to the bridge at dusk.

In an attempt to discourage wild animals from eating the other half of his food while he worked, Tree-ear had taken to hiding it closer to the house. At a far corner of Min's yard he had dug a hollow just big enough to hold the bowl, and had found a large flat rock nearby to use as a cover. It looked quite unobtrusive, and he had been pleased to find the food untouched the first time he hid it there. Since then, he had been able to bring Crane-man supper every night.

This was his greatest satisfaction. The meals provided by Min's wife were simple, but they never failed to delight his friend, who opened the gourd parcel each evening as if it were a gift of royal jewels.

'Bean curd tonight,' Crane-man would say, his eyes gleaming. 'With cucumber *kimchee* as well. Truly a felicitous combination. Soft bean curd—crunchy cucumber. Bland bean curd—spicy cucumber. That woman is an artist.'

Several days after he had begun using the new hiding place, Tree-ear made an odd discovery. As usual, he had eaten half his meal at midday. On retrieving the bowl after the day's work, he unwrapped the cloth as he always did, to check on the bowl's contents.

The bowl was full again.

Tree-ear stared in surprise. He looked towards the house, but neither Min nor his wife was in sight. And every evening thereafter he returned to find the bowl full, with enough supper for both Crane-man and himself.

Tree-ear was learning a new skill now—the draining of the clay. It was a tedious process, but one that held his interest.

At some distance from the house, near a clear running stream, a series of shallow holes had been dug and lined with several layers of rough grasscloth. The clay was shovelled into one of the pits and water mixed in to form a thick viscous mud. Tree-ear stirred and stirred the mixture with a wooden paddle until the clay and water were uniformly combined.

Then the sludge was scooped up and poured through a sieve into a neighbouring pit. The sieving winnowed out tiny pebbles and other impurities. Finally, the clay was left to settle for a few days until the water at the top either had drained away or could be bailed off.

Min would squeeze handfuls of the purified clay, or rub it between his fingers. He usually did this with his eyes closed—the better to feel it, Tree-ear supposed.

He did not ask, for Min preferred to work with as few words as possible. The potter would bark terse commands, which Tree-ear struggled to satisfy by whatever means were available to him—watching Min, watching other potters, experimenting. He did not know why Min did not explain things more fully; Tree-ear's mistakes often cost valuable time or wasted valuable clay. Then Min would shout or scold while Tree-ear stared at his toes in shame and, more often than not, resentment.

But since that first day when Tree-ear had damaged the box, Min had never raised a hand against him. Throughout the first few scoldings, Tree-ear had braced himself, ready for the pummelling that would surely follow, like those he had endured when caught raiding a rubbish heap. They had not come, then or ever, even at the height of Min's scorn and rage.

The stirring, sieving, settling, and bailing were repeated any number of times, until Min was satisfied with the residue. It depended on the job at hand. If the clay was for a sturdy teapot to be used every day, a single draining might suffice. But for a finely wrought incense burner commissioned by a wealthy merchant as a gift to the temple, the clay might be drained twice or even three times. Clay that passed Min's inspection was formed into a large ball, ready to be thrown on the wheel.

The ultimate in drainage work was reserved for the creation of the celadon glaze. For this, half a dozen drainings might not be enough. Tree-ear sometimes wanted to cry out and beat his fists into the clay in frustration when Min made an abrupt gesture for yet another repetition of the work.

The clay for glaze was mixed in precise proportions with water and wood ash. This combination must have been the result of a happy accident in the distant past. Perhaps ashes had once fallen on a plain-glazed vase in the kiln and resulted in patches of the clear celadon colour. Now potters used wood ash deliberately, each with his own secret formula, to produce the sought-after glaze.

How proud the potters were of its colour! No one had been able to name it satisfactorily, for although it was green, shades of blue and grey and violet whispered beneath it, as in the sea on a cloudy day. Different hues blended into one another where the glaze pooled thickly in the crevices or glossed sheer on the raised surfaces of an incised design. Indeed, a famed Chinese scholar had once named twelve small wonders of the world; eleven of them were Chinese, and the twelfth was the colour of Korean celadon pottery! The children of Ch'ulp'o learned this story almost before they could walk.

Tree-ear could feel the difference between the results of a first draining and that of, say, a third. After three times through the sieve, the clay was noticeably smoother, with a silky touch as light as feathers. By comparison, the residue of a first draining felt almost gravelly.

But once the process had been repeated three times, subsequent drainings did not seem to make a difference—at least, not to Tree-ear. He would squeeze his eyes shut, hold his breath, and rub the clay between his fingers, trying desperately to detect whatever was different about a fifth or sixth draining. What was it that Min felt? Why couldn't Tree-ear feel it himself?

Min never indicated any satisfaction with Tree-ear's work. He would merely pick up a ball of clay and stalk off with it towards the house. Tree-ear would stay behind to attend to the draining, resigned and envious in the knowledge that Min was taking the clay to the wheel.

In the past, keeping his ears open to the talk of village life had always been a crucial skill for Tree-ear. News of a wedding, for example, meant that the bride's family would be preparing much food in the days preceding the ceremony; their rubbish heap would merit special attention during that time. The birth of a son, the death of a patriarch—these events likewise affected the state of a household's garbage.

Of course, none of the villagers thought to tell Tree-ear of such happenings. Instead, he had learned over the years to look for the clues whispered by changes in the villagers' daily routines. Extra bags of rice delivered to one house signalled a coming feast; a normally sober man stumbling home drunk one night might mean that a son had been born.

Skipping from one rubbish heap to the next, stopping at nearly every house in the village, listening to snatches of conversation along the road—in these ways Tree-ear had come to appreciate his lowly status, for people tended to ignore his presence entirely and on the rare occasions when they did notice him, usually spoke as if he weren't there. He would carry the bits and pieces of news back to Crane-man, so they could discuss how such information might lead to a better meal.

Crane-man often joked about it. 'Tree-ear! Eh, again you see the aptness of your name. You are like the ears of a scrawny little tree, noticed by none but hearing all!'

True enough, and this ability of Tree-ear's was to serve him well in his new life as Min's assistant.

'Two months to make one vase.'

'Min, the tortoise-potter!'

'The price of one of Min's vases—two oxen, a horse, and your first-born son!'

It was thus that the other potters, their apprentices, and some of the villagers spoke of Min—usually in jest, but sometimes with derision just below the thin layer of banter in their voices. Gradually, Tree-ear learned that his master had a reputation for slow work, slow and expensive. Because he worked so slowly, he made far fewer pieces than the other potters, and consequently had to sell each of them at a higher price. Min's work was renowned for its great beauty, but there were not many who could afford it.

Tree-ear learned still more without being taught—that Min in his younger days had been one of the most successful potters in Ch'ulp'o, but that his insistence on perfection had lost him many a well-paid commission. Buyers grew tired of waiting for work that was finished months after the deadline, and eventually they took their custom elsewhere. True, there were those willing to wait for one of Min's creations, but they grew fewer every year.

Beyond all else, what Min needed was a royal commission. The everyday vessels for the king's household; the works of art displayed at the palace and its temples; and most of all, the gifts sent abroad as tokens of peace and respect to the greatest nation in the world—China . . . these were considered the worthiest of all toil, and handsomely rewarded. A royal commission was the dream of all potters, but Tree-ear sensed somehow that it was more than a dream for Min. It was his life's desire.

So Tree-ear learned about his master from others, from watching, from breathing the very air of his work, but never by hearing a word from Min himself.

*   *   *

48

The plum trees blossomed; the petals fell like snow, leaving behind tiny green buttons that hid shyly among the leaves. While Tree-ear learned to cut and drain clay, the little buttons swelled and purpled until the ripest fell to the ground, where Crane-man hopped about gathering them, the hem of his tunic tied to make a carry-sack.

That late summer Tree-ear and Crane-man always had enough to eat, for the half-empty dinner bowl never failed to become a brimful supper bowl. Tree-ear had once been tempted to eat all of the food at midday, knowing in his heart that the bowl would be refilled. But the very thought had frightened him. How quickly one became greedy! And he knew without asking that Crane-man would disapprove. Taking advantage of the kindness of another, he might say.

Instead, Tree-ear pondered long and hard how to thank Min's wife. He felt ashamed that there was so little he could do. On the rare occasions that Min dismissed him early, he would hang around the house, looking for little chores to do—pulling weeds in her vegetable patch or sweeping the yard. And he always made sure to fill the water barrel from the stream before he left for the night. His frustration at the meagreness of his thanks was like the small but constant whine of a gnat in his thoughts.

Still, it was a weightless enough worry during as fine

a time as Tree-ear could remember—golden days, warm nights, work to do, and food to eat. And Crane-man often said there was no better finish to a meal than a sweet ripe plum.

CHAPTER

5

On his way to Min's house early one morning, as the plum trees took on their gold and scarlet autumn garb, Tree-ear spied the potter Kang wheeling a cart towards the kiln site. The cart was covered over with a cloth. That in itself was of interest to Tree-ear; an ordinary commission—for a set of household bowls, say—would not merit such caution. Kang had to be firing something special that day.

Moreover, the fact that Kang was on the road so early meant that he wished to reach the kiln before anyone else. He would crawl into the oven-tunnel and push his work to the furthest end—yet another precaution against curious eyes.

Tree-ear stood still for a moment, arms crossed and brow furrowed. It seemed that it would be a good idea to visit the kiln when this particular load had finished firing.

But when he searched the kiln site several days later, Kang's work was nowhere to be found.

Over the next few days, as Tree-ear trotted about the village to and from work or on errands for Min, he kept his eyes wide in search of Kang. His vigilance was rewarded on the fourth day. Tree-ear crouched beside Kang's rubbish heap—a spot he knew well—and watched as Kang emerged from his potting shed early that evening carrying two small bowls.

Kang held them carefully, as if they were quite full. Concentrating on the bowls, he stumbled on a stone in his path. The contents of both bowls sloshed over a little, and Kang cursed loudly enough for Tree-ear to hear. Then he disappeared into the house.

Tree-ear waited a moment longer before creeping to the spot in the yard where Kang had stumbled. In the fading light, he examined the spillage closely.

Clay, mixed with enough water to be semi-liquid: the potters called it 'slip'. Nothing unusual about that. But one thing puzzled Tree-ear.

Two bowls, two different colours of slip. Brick-red and white.

Tree-ear slipped away from the yard, thinking hard.

There were places along the riverbank digging area where the clay was of various colours, to be sure. But what the potters sought was the grey-brown clay that fused so well with the celadon glaze. Both the body of a vessel and its glaze changed colour when fired; a vessel that went into the kiln a dull mousy colour emerged a remarkable translucent green.

So the diggers avoided the areas where the clay was striped dirty white or rusty red, as clay of these colours did not make the transformation to celadon green when fired. Yet Kang was working with red and white slip. What could he be doing?

Tree-ear knew that potters sometimes attempted to paint designs on their work using coloured slip. But the attempts were far from successful. When glazed and fired, the slip blurred or ran, making the edges of the design indistinct rather than crisp and clear. Every once in a while an inexperienced potter would try his hand at painting his pieces, but the more accomplished potters, Min and Kang among them, had long ago given up trying the technique.

Tree-ear did not believe that Kang was painting his pieces—but what else could one do with small amounts of coloured slip? As he walked home that evening, no answer surfaced among the questions that darted about like fish in his mind.

*   *   *

The endless cycle of work for Min continued: chopping wood, cutting clay, draining clay. Sometimes there would be a small diversion, like the time Min sent him to the beach for seashells. They were used as stilts in the kiln, to support a vessel clear of the clay stand on which it was fired, so that the two would not fuse together. The shells had to be of a precise shape and size. Tree-ear returned with a basketful of shells, of which Min rejected the majority, then sent him back for more.

Tree-ear no longer woke each morning with the thought that perhaps *this* would be the day that Min would allow him to sit at the wheel. Now he thought in moons or even seasons. Perhaps this month . . . perhaps this winter . . . or next spring. The flame of hope that burned in him was smaller now, but no less bright or fierce, and he tended it almost daily with visions of the pot he would make.

It would be a prunus vase—the most elegant of all the shapes. Tall and beautifully proportioned, rising from its base to flare gracefully and then round to the mouth, a prunus vase was designed for one purpose—to display a single branch of flowering plum.

Tree-ear loved the symmetry of the prunus vases that grew on Min's wheel. Once, back in the spring during his early days with Min, he had watched the potter place a plum branch in a finished vase to judge the effect.

The gentle curves of the vase, its mysterious green

colour. The sharp angles of the plum twigs, their blackness stark amid the airy white blossoms. The work of a human, the work of nature; clay from the earth, a branch from the sky. A kind of peace spread through Tree-ear, body and mind, as if while he looked at the vase and its branch, nothing could ever go wrong in the world.

The days shortened and grew cooler. The rice was harvested, and the poor were allowed to glean the fields for fallen grain-heads. It was an arduous, backbreaking task: hours of work to gather mere handfuls of rice. Tree-ear rose before first light now, spending an hour or so in the fields before going to work. At the end of the day he returned to the fields again, collecting rice even after darkness had rendered his eyes useless. The rice gathered now would see the poor through the winter months when no wild food grew.

There were times at the end of the day, especially, when Tree-ear thought he could not gather a single head more. *I don't really have need of it now*, he would think. But alongside that thought another would rise. *Who knows how long Min will want me to work?* And he would redouble his efforts.

Crane-man was busy, too. When he grew weary of gathering rice, he would sit at the edge of the field plaiting handfuls of rice straw to make mats and sandals. This was a skill he had taught himself long ago, being unable to perform more vigorous work because of his bad leg.

Crane-man made Tree-ear's sandals first, saying that the boy had more need of them because of his work. He measured Tree-ear's feet carefully and plaited several layers of straw for the thick, sturdy soles. More straw was cleverly twisted and woven to form the sides.

'Finished!' Crane-man exclaimed one evening, tucking in the final straw as the last of the winter light faded. He handed the pair of sandals to Tree-ear, who bowed his thanks and bent to put them on immediately.

Crane-man's face fell. Though Tree-ear jammed his foot forward and stretched the heel, the sandal was too small.

Crane-man muttered grumpily to himself and fished around in his waist pouch for the grubby string he had used to measure Tree-ear's feet. He held it up against the sole of the sandal; it was a perfect match.

He snorted. 'Ho!' he said. 'So, I did not err in the making. You, my young friend, have been so thoughtless as to grow in the last month!'

It was true; Tree-ear had noticed himself that very day, when he had bumped his head on a section of the bridge under which he had been able to stand erect before. Despite the joke, Tree-ear shook his head ruefully over Crane-man's wasted work.

And the sandals brought to mind another worry. Every

year at around this time the monks came down from their mountainside temple to collect their tithe of rice. Sometimes they accepted other donations, such as warm clothing, and Tree-ear stayed alert on the chance that a monk would pass on such garments to the poor. In this way Tree-ear had often garnered a winter wardrobe for himself and Crane-man.

This year the monks had not appeared. Perhaps there was sickness in the temple, or some other untoward event that prevented their coming, but whatever the reason, Tree-ear was growing concerned for his friend. Crane-man always suffered from the cold, and already the nights were frosty.

Soon winter rode on the back of the wind as it swept down the mountain slopes towards the village. Snow fell only rarely in Ch'ulp'o, but Tree-ear could see his every breath now, and the sharp air was full of invisible imps that bit his nose and hands and feet. It was time for Tree-ear and Crane-man to make their annual move.

During the winter the friends sheltered in a dugout on the edge of the village. The farm that once stood there had burned long ago, but the vegetable pit remained. Farmers stored vegetables for their own household use in pits the size of a room. This pit, like the others, had a sloping ramp that allowed entry. Crane-man could stand erect in the pit with his head still below ground level.

The two friends roofed the pit with tree boughs and straw. Crane-man's mats lined the floor.

Tree-ear hated the cold nights in the pit. Although he knew it was better to sleep out of the wind, being underground made him feel colder. And closed in, too—unlike the bridge, with the river a constant reminder of faraway places. If it weren't for Crane-man's presence, Tree-ear could never have borne the long winter nights.

'Not long here,' Crane-man said every year. 'The worst of winter, snowmelt, spring flood. Two moons, perhaps, and the bridge will welcome us back!'

Tree-ear waited in the yard; Min had not yet emerged from the house. When the door opened, it was his wife who appeared instead. She was holding something folded in her arms.

'Tree-ear!' she said sharply. He looked up in surprise, wondering what he had done wrong. Then he saw that though her mouth was stern, her eyes were twinkling.

'How can you work properly for the honourable potter if you are shivering with cold?' she scolded. She held out something dark and soft, and Tree-ear rose from his bow to take it from her. His eyes widened in wonder.

It was a jacket and pantaloons made of heavy cotton, quilted and padded—the warmest of garments. Min's wife took the jacket back and held it up before him.

'This should be just the right size,' she said, raising her eyebrows. Realizing what was expected of him, Tree-ear reached for and donned the jacket. A delicious cosiness enveloped him; Min's wife must have had the jacket warming by the fire inside.

'Good.' She nodded, seemed to hesitate for a moment, then spoke softly. 'Our son, Hyun-gu, died of fever when he was about your age,' she said. 'These clothes I made for him, but they were never worn.'

Tree-ear tried to swallow his surprise, but he was sure that it must have shown on his face. Min, a father? It hardly seemed possible. Tree-ear could not envision Min at anything but his work. The idea that he might once have had a son—

'Wear them in good health.' Her soft voice interrupted his thoughts, and he was suddenly aware of his discourteous behaviour. He bowed again.

'Deepest gratitude to the honourable potter's wife,' he said. She nodded again and disappeared into the house.

Min came out the next moment. He looked over Tree-ear in his new jacket. Tree-ear held his breath, wondering how Min would feel . . . his son's clothes on a lowly orphan. 'Her idea, not mine,' the potter muttered, and waved at Tree-ear to get started on his work.

Throughout the day Tree-ear kept rolling up the sleeves of the jacket, which were a little too long for him. And it made him almost too warm, accustomed as he was to hard work in his sparse burlap tunic.

So the idea was born. The jacket should fit Crane-man fairly well.

And fit it did, to Crane-man's delight. At first he refused it, saying that it was meant for Tree-ear. But Tree-ear insisted, having thought about it all the way home. Was it wrong to give away a gift that had only just been given him? It was a *gift*, he argued with himself, which meant that it was now his to do with as he pleased—to wear, or to give away. He thought of Min's wife, and decided it would not displease her if he chose to give the jacket to his friend.

Persuading Crane-man was another matter. 'If you will not wear the jacket, I will not wear the new sandals,' Tree-ear said firmly, nodding at the unfinished shoe in Crane-man's hands.

'Ha!' Crane-man shook his head. 'Stubborn monkey, I have been making you sandals every winter since you came here—and now you would refuse them?' But even as he spoke, he put on the jacket, and Tree-ear could see the pleased look beneath his scowl.

The trousers were too short for Crane-man, so Tree-ear wore those himself. They examined each other, their new garb in sharp contrast to the other rags they wore.

Crane-man began to laugh. 'Apart, we look strange enough, but together we are as properly dressed as any man!'

And he was still laughing as Tree-ear served supper from the gourd bowl.

Flickering lamplight caught Tree-ear's eye as he walked back to the pit from Min's one evening, snug in his new trousers. The days were so short now that he always came home in darkness. The light came from the shed behind Kang's house. Tree-ear paused in midstride. A light, visible from a shed with no windows—there must be a hole or a crack somewhere . . .

The temptation was too great. Tree-ear stole silently over the frozen ground, edged along the wall of the shed, and after a quick glance around, hunched over to put his eye to a shoulder-level knothole.

With the two bowls of red and white slip before him and an oil lamp just beyond, Kang sat in profile to Tree-ear's view, using his wheel as a worktable. He was working on a small wine cup. With an incising awl, he inscribed the leather-hard clay—a simple chrysanthemum design, far cruder than much of the elaborate incision work for which the potters of Ch'ulp'o were known. But rather than outlining the petals in the usual way, Kang was clearing away the clay to leave teardrop-shaped depressions.

As Tree-ear continued to watch, Kang took up a dab

of the semi-liquid white clay on the tip of the awl and deposited it into one of the petal-spaces. He repeated this action for each empty space until the white-petalled flower was clearly visible against the dull clay. For the stem and leaves he used the red clay. Then with a planing tool, he carefully smoothed away the surface of the design so that the coloured clay was completely level with the body of the vase itself.

Kang eyed his work critically, then stood and replaced the tools on a shelf. Tree-ear realized with a start that the potter must be finished for the night and would emerge from the shed any moment. He looked around warily and darted back to the road.

Tree-ear's neck and shoulders were cramped from hunching in one position for so long. As he hurried on his way, he shrugged to loosen the stiff muscles. But he might as well have been shrugging over what he had seen.

CHAPTER
6

On the days that followed, Tree-ear visited the kiln every evening in an attempt to glimpse Kang's mystery wine cup after it was fired. Once he even came upon Kang's son at the kiln, removing fired vessels and loading them onto a cart. Tree-ear pretended admiration to inspect the vessels closely. They were of ordinary celadon—no sign anywhere of the strange little chrysanthemum. By snowmelt, Tree-ear had still not seen it.

As he returned one evening from the kiln, he noticed several men and boys congregated about the wine shop. Every night there were a few who stopped by for a drink or two, but tonight there were so many that not all could fit inside. The group seemed excited about something, and one of the boys hailed him.

Tree-ear was surprised by the greeting. The other

children of Ch'ulp'o had long spurned him, for orphans were considered very bad luck. Children would step aside when he drew near, and the smaller ones often ducked behind their mothers' skirts. Since he had begun working for Min, the other potters' assistants tolerated his presence, but a friendly greeting was still a rarity. It must be important news indeed.

'Tree-ear! Have you heard? A royal emissary comes to Ch'ulp'o!'

Tree-ear moved among the clusters of people, learning bits and pieces as he listened. With winter storms over, the sea-trade routes were open again. A boat had arrived in Ch'ulp'o that afternoon; those aboard carried the news that a royal emissary would be a passenger on another boat sailing in the next moon. The emissary would be bound for Ch'ulp'o and then the district of Kangjin, a pottery region further to the south.

Ch'ulp'o and Kangjin! The two destinations could mean only one thing: The royal emissary was on a tour to assign pottery commissions for the palace!

The men drank and the boys milled about, all speculating as to how many commissions would be assigned. Nervous, fearful, impassive, serene—whatever the individual's nature, hope shouted from the face of every man, though not one spoke of his desire.

Tree-ear saw Kang in a corner of the wine shop, sitting

with his legs outstretched and his hands behind his head. Listening, saying little, his eyes half-closed and a half-smile on his face, Kang looked like nothing so much as a man with a secret.

That night Tree-ear tossed about, restlessly awake. He and Crane-man were living under the bridge again. He stared at the underside of the bridge, rolled onto his stomach, then onto his side.

Finally, Crane-man poked him. 'What demon scratches under your skin tonight?' he asked crossly. 'It seems intent on keeping us both from slumber.'

Tree-ear sat up, pulled his knees close, and wrapped his arms around them for warmth. 'A question-demon,' he said.

Crane-man sat up, too. 'Well, let us hear it, then. Perhaps if the question is asked and answered, the demon will leave you in peace—and I will be able to sleep.'

Tree-ear spoke slowly. 'It is a question about stealing.' He paused, started to speak, stopped again. Finally, 'Is it stealing to take from another something that cannot be held in your hands?'

'Ah! Not a mere question but a riddle-question, at that. What is this thing that cannot be held?'

'A—an idea. A way of doing something.'

'A better way than others now use.'

'Yes. A new way, one that could lead to great honour.'

Crane-man lay back down again. He was silent for so long that Tree-ear thought he had fallen asleep. Tree-ear sighed and lay down himself, thinking, thinking.

Min's work was far superior to Kang's. Everyone in Ch'ulp'o knew this, and Tree-ear had seen it for himself. Kang's work was skilful enough, his vessels well-shaped and his glaze a fine colour. But he lacked patience.

Firing—the final step in the process that determined the colour of the celadon—was handled well by no man. Try as the potters might, the wood in the kiln never burned the same way twice. The length of time a vessel was fired, its position in the kiln, the number of other pieces fired with it, even the way the wind blew that day—a thousand factors could affect the final colour of the glaze.

So when Min made a special piece, he prepared not one but several, sometimes as many as ten. Identical when they entered the kiln, they would emerge in slightly different colours. If all went well, one or two might glow with the desired translucent green; others would be duller or less clear. Worst of all, some of the pieces often had brown spots here and there, or even an overall tinge of brown, spoiling the purity of the glaze. No one knew why this happened, so making several identical pieces was the best safeguard to ensure that at least one would fire to an unflawed celadon green.

Not only was his work slow to begin with, but Min made more replicas than any other potter. Kang's pieces lacked Min's attention to detail in the making as well as his caution in the firing. The untrained eye might see little difference between the work of the two men—but in Ch'ulp'o, every eye was trained.

And, Tree-ear was sure, the emissary's eye would be equally sharp. The palace would send only an expert—a true connoisseur—to handle the task of commissioning work. This idea of Kang's, the use of the red and white slip . . . could it be of such newness and beauty that it would mean a commission? If that were indeed the case, Tree-ear had no doubt that Min could use the process to far better effect.

But Min did not know about it. And therein lived the question-demon: If Tree-ear were to tell Min what he had seen, would that be stealing Kang's idea?

Crane-man's voice startled Tree-ear.

'If a man is keeping an idea to himself, and that idea is taken by stealth or trickery—I say it is stealing. But once a man has revealed his idea to others, it is no longer his alone. It belongs to the world.'

Tree-ear did not reply. He lay curled on one side, listening as Crane-man's breathing slowed and evened in the rhythm of sleep.

An image floated out of the darkness into Tree-ear's

mind—that of himself with his eye pressed to the knot-hole of Kang's shed.

Stealth.

He could not yet tell Min of Kang's idea.

Tree-ear's activities in the days that followed were no different than they had been for months. Min and the other potters continued throwing pots, incising them with designs, glazing, firing, rejecting some vessels and keeping others. But things felt different to Tree-ear—the smallest of changes here and there.

Min no longer sang at the wheel. His wife, normally almost invisible as she went about her household tasks, emerged from the house more often, sometimes to watch her husband at work for a moment, at other times to give him a cup of tea or a rice cake, as he now worked right through the midday mealtime. At the kiln the potters no longer joked among themselves or smoked idly. Instead, they paced about in restless silence.

All went about their work with their faces tighter, as if the news of the emissary's impending visit had pulled the string of village life taut.

By unspoken agreement, Tree-ear joined the other potters' assistants one morning in the area between the beach and the village that served as a market place. They picked up debris, swept the space clear, and set up planks to display their masters' wares. Tree-ear glanced surreptitiously at his colleagues; many were setting up half a dozen planks or more. For Min, only two such planks would be needed. As usual, he would have by far the fewest pieces to display.

Min's instructions had been explicit. Tree-ear was to set up the stall so that Min would stand with his back to the sea and his wares before him. The emissary would thus be facing the sea when he inspected Min's work. Though Min did not explain, Tree-ear knew why. It was so the emissary would see how Min's vessels captured the elusive green and blue and grey hues of the waves.

The boat docked one evening at sunset. The emissary and his entourage spent the night at the home of the local government official. Tree-ear guessed that if those in the royal party slept that night, they were the only ones in Ch'ulp'o who did so. Long before dawn the market space was lit by dozens of oil lamps as potters and their assistants rushed about in an anxious, eerie silence, preparing their stalls.

Tree-ear wheeled the cart down the road from Min's house—a step at a time, or so it seemed. The potter walked by his side, keeping up a constant stream of warnings and invective.

'Watch that stone there, to the left! Keep the cart even, stupid boy. This way—the path is smoother here. *Ai-go!*

What's the matter with you? Can't you keep it from bumping for even one second? You will ruin my work, pig-head!'

Min's vessels were muffled in layers and layers of tightly packed rice straw; Tree-ear thought grimly that even if he ran at full speed, no harm would come to the work. At least his master's limited output meant that only one such trip would be necessary.

At last, they arrived at the makeshift stall. Min would not allow Tree-ear to unload the cart or unpack the vessels. Instead, he was ordered to pick up every scrap of straw on the ground.

Min arranged his work with great care. On the higher of the two shelves, he placed the smaller pieces. There was the little duck-shaped water dropper, and another one in the form of a lotus bud. They were flanked by three incense burners whose basins were surmounted by animals nearly alive in their detail—roaring lion, fierce dragon, wise tortoise. And in the centre was a new set of nested boxes, inscribed with a splendid floral design. Tree-ear had learned the answer to their mystery: Min used thin slabs of clay to build the small interior boxes first, then the larger one to fit around them.

On the lower shelves, Min placed two prunus vases, a tall jug ribbed like a melon, and a water pot in its matching bowl. This last piece was a special favourite of Tree-ear's.

70

The bowl was covered with moulded petals that over-lapped one another—and held a secret.

Tree-ear had watched his master make dozens of those petals and had finally taken a small lump of clay home in his waist pouch to practise himself. After many evenings of work he had produced a single petal that he thought as fine as one of Min's.

Now, as he looked at the pot, shame clashed with pride inside him. For he had taken his petal the next day and secretly substituted it for another among those drying on Min's shelf. His act had gone undetected. The stealth of it shamed him—but not enough to overcome the pride he felt at the knowledge that one of the many petals on the bowl was his. And best of all, though he had examined the piece closely a dozen times, he could not tell which it was.

Min stood before the display of his wares, shaking his head and clucking with discontent. He muttered under his breath—the glaze of one piece was not as fine as it could have been, he should have made one more duck. Oh, everything was well enough, but if he had had more time . . .

As Tree-ear looked over the shelves, an idea came to him. He bowed to Min and begged his leave for a short moment; Min waved him off, hardly seeming to hear him.

Tree-ear raced through the village all the way to the scrub behind Min's house. He found what he needed and hurried back, but not so quickly this time, so as to protect what he carried.

Out of breath, he arrived back at the market space.

'Master,' he panted, and held out his offering—two branches of flowering plum. Tree-ear thought that Min looked pleased for the briefest instant; then his usual cross expression returned as he took the branches.

'Hmph. Yes, it would do well to show the vases as they should be used.' Min examined the branches, then handed one back to Tree-ear.

'That branch does not have enough blossoms. Why did you not bring more?' And he turned his back on Tree-ear to arrange the other branch in the vase on the left.

Tree-ear grinned. He knew his master well enough now, and Min's response was as close as he would ever come to expressing pleasure at Tree-ear's work.

There was yet one task remaining for Tree-ear before the emissary arrived, and it was not a task assigned by Min. Now that the display was complete, Tree-ear sought out Kang's stall.

Every potter was busy, but a small group had still taken the time to visit Kang's display. Even from a distance,

Tree-ear could sense their suppressed interest, though none there spoke beyond a word or two. Tree-ear approached as if merely passing by, but his very skin prickled with curiosity.

Then a space before the stall cleared as a man stepped away, and Tree-ear saw them.

Chrysanthemums.

Dozens of them. On every vessel—blooming from wine cups and jugs and vases and bowls—the simple eight-petalled flowers caught one's attention and seized it as if they would never let go. The slight imperfections of Kang's vessels disappeared in the light that seemed to blaze from the pure-white blossoms.

Tree-ear stepped closer. He saw that a few of the pieces had stem and leaf as well. But they were no longer brick-red. In the firing, the red slip had turned black, and the contrast of black and white against jade green was unmistakably new, different, remarkable.

And beautiful. Even as Tree-ear turned away, feigning disinterest, as were the other potters, his heart was sinking into a bottomless well. The technique was so striking that the emissary could not help but choose Kang for a commission—Tree-ear was sure of it.

Emissary Kim was a tall, thoughtful man who showed no emotion as he walked from stall to stall inspecting the work of every potter. At some displays he took more time;

73

the potters' hopes rose a little higher with every second he examined their wares.

He spent the longest time at Kang's stall, and the other potters gave up all pretence of indifference. They gathered around at a respectful distance as the emissary spoke with Kang.

Inlay work, Kang explained. The same as was done to apply brass to wood or mother-of-pearl to lacquerware. Kim nodded along with those in the little audience; inlay work was common enough in other arts, but no one there had ever seen it used in ceramics before.

Kang gave no other details of the technique; nor did the emissary request any. He merely took a great deal of time to inspect Kang's pieces thoroughly. Tree-ear felt a flicker of hope when he saw that Kim looked not only at the chrysanthemums but at every aspect of the work. At last, he replaced the vase he was holding and, still expressionless, moved on to the next stall.

It seemed to Tree-ear that he would never reach Min's stall—yet when he did, it was all too soon.

Kim immediately picked up the melon-shaped jug and looked it over with keen interest. For the first time the planes of his face shifted—with pleasure? Tree-ear could not tell.

'Would this be the potter who made the wine pot used at last night's dinner?' The emissary addressed the question to Yee, the local government official at whose home he had spent the night. Yee was one of several men accompanying Kim on his inspection of the potters' work. He nodded in reply.

'The melon shape is common enough now—I see it often,' Kim said. Tree-ear could hardly breathe. Did this mean that the man did not care for the piece?

'And yet this work is unmistakable,' he continued. 'I knew this jug could be by no other than the same man who made that pot.' And suddenly the expression on his face seemed pleased.

Min bowed in appreciation of the compliment, and Tree-ear wondered at his master's calm; he himself had to still the glee that surged through him, lest it make him skip about, shouting. Kim took his time looking over Min's work and finally walked on to the next display.

Despite the emissary's apparent pleasure, Tree-ear knew there would be no decision that day. Kim would spend a few more days in Ch'ulp'o, visiting the potters whose work most interested him, perhaps stopping by the kiln site occasionally. Then he would sail on to Kangjin. Only after he had visited both villages would he decide which potters were to receive commissions. His selections were to be announced the following month on his return visit.

After the emissary's departure, Ch'ulp'o was like two villages instead of one. The potters whose work had garnered special attention, including both Min and Kang, burst into feverish activity in an effort to make one last piece that might sway a decision in their favour when Kim returned. The other potters seemed to slump as one into dejection, all but abandoning their work in favour of long, lugubrious visits to the wine shop, where they commiserated with one another.

For they knew well that royal commissions were assigned at seemingly random intervals. Potters so chosen worked for as long as their art continued to please the court; for most, a commission would last the rest of their lives. Only when a potter died or his work fell out of favour was a new commission assigned. And often the court waited until the demise of two or three potters before searching out their replacements. It could be many years before such a chance came again.

CHAPTER

7

Min was far more irritable than usual after the emissary's visit. Instead of giving gruff, terse commands, he harangued Tree-ear at every opportunity. Then he would lapse into a sullen silence that lasted until his next bout of shouting.

Tree-ear worked harder than ever, tense with anticipation. Min was making vases in the melon shape that had so pleased the emissary. It seemed to Tree-ear that the potter had never before rejected so many pieces that came off the wheel; all day long, to the tune of Min's curses he heard the sound of clay being slapped down in disgust.

At last, after two days of abuse, Min asked the question Tree-ear had been waiting for.

'So,' Min said grumpily, 'would you be telling me about it, or must I guess?'

Min was the only potter who had not visited Kang's display that day. Whether genuine or feigned, his concentration on his own work had never wavered, but Tree-ear knew he could not have failed to notice the gathering of people, the air that had ruffled with interest around Kang's stall.

'Inlay work,' Tree-ear responded at once. Crane-man's words echoed in his mind. *The idea belongs to the world now.* He continued, 'White and red slip that fires to white and black in the finish. Chrysanthemums.'

Min did not reply, so Tree-ear added, 'Ugly ones.'

For what Tree-ear guessed was the first time in Min's whole life, the potter threw back his head in a loud guffaw of laughter.

'Ha!' he spat out, choked, cleared his throat. He looked at Tree-ear with what might have almost been affection. 'Ugly ones, you say? Of course! What else could Kang do, that bumble-fingered excuse for a potter?' Suddenly, he clapped his hands once and snapped, 'Go, then. White and red clay, drained, as for glaze.'

Tree-ear jumped to his feet. Almost before Min had finished speaking, he was flying down the road with the cart careering crazily before him.

Days before, Tree-ear had mapped out the best places along the river for coloured clay, and now he went directly to the first spot. He dug and loaded, his excitement kept in check by the rhythm of the work. The spade had never felt so light as it did that day.

Over the next several days, Min sketched what seemed like hundreds of designs. His wife helped by drawing the basic melon shape over and over in charcoal on pieces of wood. Min would add his ideas for the inlay design, reject them angrily, and hand the wood back to her to be wiped and reused.

Meanwhile, Tree-ear was busy draining the clay. Twice, three times, four—and the fifth time with the white clay, something happened.

Tree-ear was rubbing the sediment between his fingers, as he always did. Suddenly, his fingertips tingled with a strange feeling. For some odd reason, he thought of a time when he had been on the mountainside, taking a break as he chopped wood. He had been staring into the forest greenery when a deer appeared in abrupt focus. It had been there all along, and he had been looking straight at it. But only at the last moment had he actually *seen* it.

It was the same now, only instead of seeing with his eyes, he was feeling with his hands. The clay felt good— fine, pliant, smooth—*but not ready yet*.

Tree-ear froze, completely still except for the tips of his fingers in the clay. What was it that made him think so? His mind could not find the right words. The clay had long since lost any feeling of roughness, but somehow he knew. *One more draining—perhaps two . . .* It was like suddenly seeing the deer—a clear vision emerging from a cloudy dream.

And it was as if he woke from that dream as he drained the clay yet again—a dream in which the words to describe exactly how he knew about the clay would be held secret forever.

Having finally selected a design, Min began incising it. This was the most detailed part of the work, and he disliked anyone watching. As Tree-ear swept the yard or brought clay to and from the draining site, he tried to catch what glimpses he could. It was always so when Min was incising; now that Tree-ear knew well every aspect of Min's work, he loved seeing the incision work emerge even more than he had once loved watching the vessels grow on the wheel.

Min used sharp tools with points of various sizes. The outline of the design was first etched lightly into the leather-hard clay with the finest point. Then Min would carve out the design a bit at a time. Unlike other potters, who traced a complete pattern with their initial incisions, Min sometimes varied from the sketchy tracing; his work seemed to flow more freely both in the making and in the final result.

The glaze would collect in the crevices of the design,

making it slightly darker than the rest of the surface. Once the piece was fired, the pattern would be so subtle as to be almost invisible in some kinds of light. Min's incision work was meant to provide a second layer of interest, another pleasure for the eye, without detracting in the least from the grace of shape and wonder of colour that were a piece's first claims to beauty.

Min was inscribing lotus blossoms and peonies between the ribbed lines of one of the melon vases. At the end of each day, Tree-ear always tried to check Min's shelves, to see what progress had been made. Because Min was now attempting inlay work, rather than merely incision, some of the petal and leaf spaces were carved out into little depressions. But Tree-ear could already see how much finer and more detailed Min's work was than Kang's. The blossoms had many more petals, each beautifully shaped; the stems and leaves twined and feathered as if alive.

Tree-ear exulted silently over his master's work. He could hardly wait to see the pieces after they were fired. Surely, the emissary would see that Min's work could both honour tradition and welcome the new in a way that was worthy of a commission.

Min came to the draining site after a few days to check on Tree-ear's work. Because only small amounts were needed, Tree-ear was working with the red and white clay in bowls instead of in the pits. Min closed his eyes as he touched his fingertips to the contents of one bowl.

After a brief instant, he opened his eyes and sniffed. 'You took long enough,' he said dismissively. He walked back to the house carrying both bowls.

Tree-ear pressed his lips together so as not to grin too widely at the potter's departing back. It was the first time he had prepared the clay to such a fine finish without further prompting from Min.

Min made five replicas of the melon-shaped vase. To inscribe the design and then inlay each part of it with the coloured slip was the work of countless hours, and Tree-ear remained at the house until well after dark to assist Min however he could. After a vase had been inscribed and inlaid, Min removed every bit of excess slip. Finally, the vases were dipped in glaze. Never had Tree-ear taken such care over the draining, and Min himself had done the final drainings and mixing of the glaze.

Min was like a man with a demon inside him. He ate little, slept less, and whether he worked by daylight or lamplight, his eyes always seemed to glitter with ferocity. Tree-ear felt that the very air in the workspace under the eaves was alive with whispers and hisses of anxiety: the emissary would be returning very soon.

At last, the day came when they would load the vases into the kiln. Each vase was placed carefully on three seashells set in a triangle atop one of the clay shelves, in a position near the middle of the kiln where Min determined it would fire best. Then the wood was precisely arranged in a complicated crisscross pattern of many layers. The kindling of twigs and pine needles was lit with a spark from a flint stone, and when the fire was well on its way, the door of the kiln was sealed.

The heat in the kiln was extremely difficult to control. The kiln had to heat up slowly—too rapid a rise in temperature at the start, and the vessels would crack. This warming process took a full day. Beginning on the second day, more wood was added from time to time through openings in the kiln walls. On the third or fourth day, when a potter hoped that the correct temperature had been reached, the openings were sealed with clay plugs. The fire blazed at its hottest then, until it had eaten all the air within the kiln and began to die. And it took two or three days for the kiln to cool down.

Min preferred to fire his replicas in at least two different batches whenever possible. But with the emissary's return nearly at hand, there was time for only one firing.

While Min always stayed at the kiln during the crucial first stages of warming and adding more fuel, he usually went home after the openings had been sealed. This time, however, he remained at the site for the entire period of the firing. Tree-ear laid armfuls of straw on the hillside, and there Min sat, the hollows under his eyes dark with exhaustion. His orders were curt, as usual, but quiet.

Tree-ear could hardly believe it; he would almost rather have Min shouting at him. The quiet was alarming. Tree-ear brought food from the house, but Min left most of his untouched. He sent Tree-ear back and forth between the house and the kiln on various errands. At the end of each day Tree-ear crept away on tiptoe, as if any noise might disrupt Min's concentration and somehow ruin the firing.

Tree-ear had never figured out if it was his footfalls that woke Crane-man, or if Crane-man simply did not sleep until Tree-ear came home. But no matter how late it was, his friend never failed to greet him when he arrived under the bridge. Nor was his voice ever weighed down with sleep.

Tree-ear's long hours of work for Min left the two friends no time or light for walks or other activities; instead, Crane-man had taken to telling stories. He had often told folk-tales—of foolish donkeys or brave tigers—when Tree-ear was a youngster. But that had been some years ago, and Tree-ear welcomed the chance to hear the old yarns again. There were new ones, too, sagas about the heroes and heroines of Korea. The stories were a much-needed distraction; after listening to Crane-man's voice for a while, Tree-ear was able to relax and fall into a dreamless sleep.

On the last day, Min told Tree-ear to spend the afternoon at the house, tidying the yard. He was to return to the site after sundown. The pieces would be removed from the kiln under cover of darkness.

A misted half-moon had risen to the height of its arc by the time Tree-ear had swept the kiln entrance clear of ashes. Holding a lamp, he stood aside as Min crawled in. Min used a pair of special wooden tongs to carry out the still-hot vases one by one, and placed them carefully into the cart, where Tree-ear had prepared a bed of straw. The moon did not give enough light for Tree-ear to see clearly, but when the last vase had been removed, Tree-ear crawled back into the kiln to fetch the lamp.

The flame in the small lamp flickered treacherously; it was difficult to inspect the vases closely. The inlay work stood out even in the deceptive light. But Min sighed and shook his head. They would have to wait until morning to see the results.

Together they packed more straw between the vases. Then Min held the lamp while Tree-ear cautiously rolled the cart back to the house, the night quiet except for the single-minded singing of the frogs by the river and, once, the plaintive call of a night bird.

'You are late tonight, my friend,' Crane-man called, lighting the lamp as Tree-ear slid down the embankment.

'Unloading the kiln,' Tree-ear replied. 'I am sorry you had to wait so long for your supper.'

Crane-man waved his crutch as if brushing away the apology. 'I eat too well these days. Fat and lazy, that's what I have become,' he joked.

Tree-ear should have been nearly dead with fatigue, but he was too tense to lie down. Instead, he sat up and watched his friend eat. As the light flickered around the little den formed by the bridge overhead and the river-bank walls, Tree-ear suddenly had the sense of seeing clearly the things that had always been there. Like the deer with his eyes, or the clay with his fingers . . .

The few cooking pots and bowls were stacked on a little shelf formed by the rocks, with chopsticks, a single spoon, and Crane-man's knife in a neat row. Tree-ear's sleeping mat was rolled up and set to one side. There were two baskets Crane-man had woven. One held a few wild mushrooms; the other, bits and pieces that might come in handy one day—scraps of cloth, twine, flint stone. Everything was so familiar to Tree-ear. Crane-man having lived under the bridge so many more years, it must be nearly invisible to him by now.

Tree-ear spoke almost before he thought. 'Crane-man—how is it that when you lost your home and your family, you did not go to the temple?'

Those with nowhere else to go always went to the temple.

The monks took them in, fed them, gave them work to do. Eventually, many of them became monks themselves. This would have been the usual course for someone who met with misfortune as Crane-man had, and Tree-ear wondered why he had never asked the question before.

Crane-man looked almost displeased for an instant; then his lips curled into a sheepish smile. 'Ah. There is a reason, but it is a foolish one, and would become more so in the telling.'

Tree-ear waited.

'Psshh,' Crane-man said at last. 'It is a worse foolishness to do something foolish and then to be unable to laugh at it later! A fox, then. It was a fox that kept me from the temple.'

'A fox?'

Foxes were dreaded animals. They were not large or fierce, like the bears and tigers that roamed the mountains, but they were known to be fiendishly clever. Some people even believed that foxes possessed evil magic. It was said that a fox could lure a man to his doom, tricking him into coming to its den, where somehow he would be fed to its offspring.

Even to say the word made a trickle of fear run down Tree-ear's spine.

'The house had been sold,' Crane-man said. 'I gathered up my few things and made ready to go to the temple. It was a fine day, I remember, and I made a long time of it, walking up the mountainside.

'So it was dusk, and I was still a good distance away. Suddenly, a fox appeared before me. It stopped there, right in the middle of the path, grinning with all its teeth shining white, licking its lips, its eyes glowing, its broad tail swishing back and forth slowly, back and forth—'

'Enough!' Tree-ear's eyes were wide with horror. 'What happened?'

Crane-man picked up the last morsel of rice with his chopsticks and popped it into his mouth. 'Nothing,' he said. 'I have come to believe that foxes could not possibly be as clever as we think them. There I was, close enough to touch one, with a bad leg as well—and here I still am today.

'But that night, of course, I could not continue on my journey. I walked all the way down the mountain again, looking over my shoulder nearly the whole time. The fox did not follow me; indeed, it disappeared as quickly as it had come. That night I stayed under the bridge, although you can be sure that I found no sleep.

'It was many days before I could even think about making the journey again, and by that time, this'—Crane-man waved his chopsticks at the little space—'had begun to seem like home. Days became months, months grew into years. Then you came along.' Crane-man smiled as he finished his story. 'Between the fox and you, I was destined never to become a monk!'

Tree-ear unrolled his sleeping mat and lay down. But a few moments later he rose to his knees and peered at the darkness beyond the bridge. Were those two eyes glowing—or just reflections of starlight on the river?

As always, Crane-man seemed to know what Tree-ear was doing even in the dark. 'Go to sleep!' he ordered, sounding almost like Min. 'Or are you trying to make me feel an even bigger fool for planting foolishness in you?'

Tree-ear shook his head, smiling, and settled down at last.

To Tree-ear's surprise, Min's wife was waiting for him out on the road in front of the house the next morning. Beside her were the cart and spade. Although her face was as placid and kind as always, Tree-ear saw in her eyes some great worry that even her gentle smile of greeting could not hide.

'More clay, Tree-ear,' she said quietly. 'Both plain and coloured.'

Tree-ear bowed in reply, and she turned back to the house. He trotted down the road a few paces, until he was sure she had gone inside. Then he left the cart by the side of the road and crept around to the back of the house.

Tree-ear felt the blood drain from his face at the terrible sight that greeted his eyes. The yard was covered with pieces of shattered pottery—hundreds of them, it seemed.

Tree-ear knew at once what had happened—the face of Min's wife had told him. She was neither angry nor fearful; instead, she had seemed deeply, quietly, sad. It could mean only one thing. Min had smashed the vases himself.

Tree-ear counted on his fingers—five piles of shards, all five of the melon-shaped vases. One of them had been hurled so far that pieces of it lay just a few paces short of where he stood peeping from behind the corner of the house. Tree-ear glanced about quickly, then tiptoed a few steps into the yard and gathered up some of the larger pieces. He tucked them hastily into his waist pouch and darted back to the cart.

At the riverbank Tree-ear lowered the cart handles and reached inside his waist pouch for the shards of pottery. The inlay work was flawless, the floral design intricate and graceful even on the incomplete pieces he held. But the glaze . . . Tree-ear frowned and squinted.

The dreaded brown tint suffused the glaze of every piece; some of them were marred with brown spots as well. They were fragments of the same vase, but the destruction of all five meant that every vase was flawed. Min had done the mixing of the glaze himself, so the mistake could only have been in the firing—the part of the work over which not even Min had complete control.

Tree-ear gripped the shards tightly. He cried out as he flung them into the river, not even noticing that one of them had cut his palm.

There was no time left. Even now the emissary's boat might be in the harbour.

CHAPTER
8

Min began work on another set of inlaid vases. But before the throwing was complete, the emissary's ship docked. Emissary Kim sent a messenger to ask if any of the potters had anything new to show. Min waved the messenger away without a word.

The next morning the news blew through the village like a sudden sea breeze: The emissary had visited Kang's house. Kang had been chosen for a commission.

Later that morning Tree-ear swept up the remains of the destroyed vases in Min's yard. It was as he had guessed—all of the pieces bore traces of brown clouded glaze. Tree-ear felt numb with disappointment; he wondered how much worse it must be for Min.

The potter had still not come out of the house with instructions for the day, so Tree-ear turned to the vegetable patch. He squatted down and began to pull the first of a thousand noxious shoots that threatened the cucumber plants so precious to Min's wife.

Someone called out from the front of the house; Tree-ear recognized the voice of the government official Yee.

'Potter Min! The emissary is here. He wishes to speak with you.'

Tree-ear dropped the ragged weed he was holding and stole around to the window at the side of the house. He could see little but heard everything. Min welcomed Yee, Emissary Kim, and the men of the royal cortège into his home. They sat around a low table in silence. Tree-ear heard the clink of pottery as Min's wife served tea.

Then Emissary Kim began to speak. 'This inlay work of your colleague's. It is something new, and will be of great interest to the court.'

There was a pause; Tree-ear imagined Min nodding in polite agreement.

'I will speak with no veil over my thoughts, Potter Min. Other aspects of Potter Kang's work are—how can I say it?—not as much to my taste. Kang has been given what I will call a limited commission. He will produce work for the court for a year, to see if it pleases His Majesty.'

Kim hesitated, then continued. 'I would far rather have given you the honour of a royal commission. But I would be remiss in my responsibilities if I were to ignore this new technique. It must be presented to the court.

'I will now return to Songdo. But if you were to produce something using this inlay style, and bring it to me in Songdo, I would guarantee a careful consideration of the work.'

Tree-ear could barely contain his excitement. *The shards!* he wanted to shout. *Show him the pieces from the rubbish heap! He is an expert—he will understand about the firing.*

But Min was speaking now. 'The royal emissary honours me with his words, and I wish to disappoint no one. But I am an old man now. I could not possibly make the journey to Songdo. I thank the emissary for his consideration and beg his understanding for my failure.'

Tree-ear heard the swish of fine heavy fabric as the emissary rose to his feet and went to the door. The emissary spoke once more.

'It is my wish that you find a way somehow, Potter Min. It would be a great sorrow to me if this were to be the last time I saw your fine work.' Then he and his entourage were gone.

Tree-ear turned and slid down the wall, slumped over with his head in his hands. *The old fool!* he thought. *He does not wish the emissary to see the imperfect glaze . . . his pride keeps him from a royal commission. The fool . . .*

Just then Min's wife came around the house with a basket of laundry. Tree-ear jumped to his feet to help her. She nodded her thanks, calm as ever, as if the tumultuous events of the past few days had never happened. They stood on either side of the clothes line; he handed her the garments and she hung them. Her serenity and the rhythm of the task helped soothe Tree-ear's raw nerves.

Yet again he wished he could think of a way to show his gratitude for her kindness. What was it she wanted? he wondered. She seemed to have no desires of her own . . . or perhaps her wishes were those of her husband's.

Suddenly, an answer came to Tree-ear as if calling from the clear sky.

Doing Min a favour—a great favour—that was the way to thank her. Her husband's success—that was what she desired. Before he could think about it any longer, he heard himself speaking.

'I have a request to make of the honourable potter's wife,' he said.

'Please,' she replied.

'I—I am aware of the generous offer made by the royal emissary,' he confessed, and glanced quickly at her. Her eyes crinkled in amusement, so he knew she did not mind that he had eavesdropped.

'If the master would make a vessel he considers worthy

95

of the court's attention, it would be my greatest honour to be allowed to take it to Songdo for him.'

Her face was partially hidden behind the linen sheet she was hanging; she fixed it firmly to the line before she answered.

'I will ask the master, under one condition,' she said. 'No, two conditions. The first is that you return to Ch'ulp'o quickly and safely.'

Tree-ear bowed, puzzled. Why should it matter to her how he journeyed?

'And the second . . .' She paused. 'The second is that from now on, you will call me *Ajima*.'

Tree-ear's eyes filled with tears. He bent to pick up another piece of laundry. *Ajima* meant something like 'Auntie'; it was a term of great affection, reserved only for older kinswomen. Tree-ear was kin to no one, and yet Min's wife wished for him to call her Ajima. He did not even know if he could say the word.

'Well, Tree-ear?' The gentle teasing had returned to her voice. 'Do you agree to my conditions?'

Tree-ear nodded. He spoke from behind the clothes that flapped on the line. 'I agree,' he said, then faltered. His voice fell to a whisper. 'I agree—Ajima.'

A few days later, Tree-ear crouched under the bridge, watching idly as Crane-man shaved another sliver of wood from the chopstick he was whittling. Without looking up, Crane-man said, 'It is too bad that your thoughts are not on a string. If they were, I would have given them a good yank by now—to see what I could see.'

Tree-ear chewed on the inside of his cheek. He should have known it was folly to keep a secret from Crane-man, even for a few days.

'I will be going on a journey soon,' Tree-ear said. He meant to speak firmly, but his voice sounded loud and coarse instead.

'A journey, eh?' Crane-man continued whittling. 'It is a good thing for a man to see the world if he can. Where will you go?'

Two days before, Min had handed Tree-ear some tools to be cleaned, saying, 'The vessels will be finished by midsummer. If you leave then, you will be able to return before the snow.' In this way Tree-ear learned that Min was sending him to Songdo.

Since that moment Tree-ear had regretted the rashness of his offer. He had never once left Ch'ulp'o since his arrival as a toddler. How could he possibly think of making such a journey? It would take many days, over unfamiliar mountains where there might not even be a path to follow, much less a road. He might well lose his way. And who knew what perils awaited him? Robbers, wild animals, rockslides . . . What had he been thinking?

97

But, then, what was he to do—tell Min he had changed his mind?

No. Going to Songdo was hardly possible, but not going was worse.

'Min has some work that must be transported—for an audience at the royal court.'

Crane-man put down his knife, leaned back, and crossed his arms. 'An audience at the court? Why the riddle-talk, my friend? Why do you not say, "I am going to the capital—to Songdo"?'

Tree-ear swallowed. He rose to his feet and walked the few steps to the water's edge, picked up a flat stone, and threw it so it skipped across the water. Four times it lit on the surface; how was it that a stone could be so like a bird?

Crane-man stood, too, and skipped a stone of his own. Six touches. Tree-ear shrugged as a little smile stretched his lips. In all the years under the bridge he had never once defeated Crane-man at this game. Together they watched until the ripples from the stone had melted away.

'I am going to—to Songdo,' Tree-ear said at last, as if testing the words. He looked at his companion pleadingly. 'It seems too far away, to say it.'

'No, my friend,' Crane-man said. 'It is only as far as the next village. A day's walk, on your young legs.'

Tree-ear frowned, mystified. But before he could speak,

Crane-man continued. 'Your mind knows that you are going to Songdo. But you must not tell your body. It must think one hill, one valley, one day at a time. In that way, your spirit will not grow weary before you have even begun to walk.

'One day, one village. That is how you will go, my friend.'

Tree-ear watched as Crane-man stirred up the water with his crutch a little. Then he raised the dripping crutch and pointed it at Tree-ear.

'Off you go now, to bring me some straw. You will need some extra sandals for such a journey, and who is to make them if not I?'

Min spent his time on the new set of vases, one or two of which would be selected to be taken to Songdo. In the meantime, the pace had slowed considerably for Tree-ear. So frenetically had he worked during the time surrounding the emissary's visits that he was ahead of schedule on all his tasks. Plenty of wood filled the shed at the kiln site; balls of clay and bowls of slip awaited Min's need. Tree-ear found himself idle on occasion, with too much time to think.

And think he did, gathering his courage until at last there was enough of it to enable him to stand before Min with a request.

'What is it now?' Min asked. Tree-ear had lingered by the house at the end of the day, waiting for Min to look up from the wheel.

'Master.' Tree-ear bowed. 'It is now more than a year that I have had the honour of working for you.'

'A year . . . yes. So?'

Tree-ear pulled in the muscles of his stomach to stop their quaking. 'I was wondering . . . if the Master would be so good . . . if he thinks my work worthy—'

Min snapped, 'Ask your question or leave me in peace, boy!'

'If you would one day be teaching me to make a pot.' Tree-ear's words rushed out in a single breath.

Min sat motionless for a long moment—long enough for Tree-ear to wonder if perhaps his request had been unclear. At last, Min stood and Tree-ear raised his head.

'Know this, orphaned one,' Min said slowly. 'If ever you learn to make a pot, it will not be from me.'

Tree-ear could not stop himself. 'Why?' he cried out. 'Why will you not teach me?'

Min picked up the half-formed vessel before him and slammed it back onto the wheel with such force that Tree-ear flinched.

'Why?' Min repeated. 'I will tell you why.' The potter's voice was low, but shook with the effort of control. 'The

100

potter's trade goes from father to son. I had a son once. My son, Hyun-gu. He is gone now. It is him I would have taught. You—'

Tree-ear saw the potter's eyes, fierce with grief and rage. Min choked out the last words: 'You are not my son.'

CHAPTER

9

Tree-ear could hardly breathe on his walk home. Min's words rang in his ears, over and over: *orphaned one . . . father to son . . . not my son.* He realized now what he had never thought to notice before: All the other apprentices were indeed sons of the potters.

It's not my fault! Tree-ear wanted to shout. He wanted to run all the way back to Min and scream the words. *It's not my fault you lost your son, not my fault that I am an orphan! Why must it be father to son? If the pot is made well, does it matter whose son made it?*

Crane-man hailed him cheerfully from under the bridge with the news that two pairs of sandals were complete. Tree-ear feigned eagerness as he tried them on, but he knew that Crane-man had read his troubled face at once. Crane-man said nothing, only waited.

Tree-ear tied the sandals together carefully in pairs. As he hung them up in a safe place under the bridge, he said, 'The potter's trade passes from father to son here in Ch'ulp'o. Is it thus everywhere?'

'A story tells the answer to that,' Crane-man replied. He hobbled over to a large rock and sat down. Tree-ear knelt beside him.

'Potters have not always been considered artists, you know. In the long-ago days when potters made objects for use and not beauty, it was considered a poor trade indeed. None wished for their sons to have such a lowly life.

'Year after year, more sons left the trade until at last there were not enough potters to supply the needs of the people! So the king at the time decreed that sons of potters must become potters themselves.'

Tree-ear shook his head and even managed a grim smile. Imagine, sons running away from what he wished most to do!

'I do not know if it is still a law,' Crane-man continued. 'But a well-kept tradition can be stronger than law.'

Tree-ear nodded. At least he knew now that it would be useless to leave Ch'ulp'o in search of another master.

Crane-man stood and leaned on his crutch to stretch out his good leg. He glanced sideways at Tree-ear. 'My friend, the same wind that blows one door shut often blows another open,' he said.

Tree-ear stood, too, and went to fetch the supper bowl. It sometimes took him a while to figure out Crane-man's riddles, but he preferred puzzling over them to being told what they meant.

Work no longer felt the same to Tree-ear. He now realized that he had been working all along towards the goal of being allowed to make a pot. With that hope gone, so went his eagerness to work. More than ever, he wished that he had not been so rash as to offer to take Min's vessels to Songdo. He would do it—not for the old potter, he thought bitterly, but for Ajima.

Tree-ear checked the clay at the draining site. Some of the clay balls were drying out too quickly; he dampened the cloths that covered them. Then, using a wooden blade, he scored the surface of the clay in the drainage bed so it would dry faster. How much slower the work went when the joy of it was gone.

The clay in the bed was coming along well; it would be ready to form into balls soon. Tree-ear took up a handful of clay from the corner of the bed and kneaded it. Absent-mindedly, he began to form a petal shape. After so many attempts at making the petal that was eventually used for the water pot, his hands seemed to work of their own accord, flattening here, pinching there . . .

Tree-ear's hands paused in midmotion. Slowly he brought the half-formed petal up to eye level and examined it closely.

Moulding, he thought. There was more than one way to make a piece of pottery. Throwing, of course—using the wheel to assist in shaping a symmetrical piece. But the little animals atop the incense burners, the handles of some vessels, the water droppers—they were not thrown. They were moulded by hand without any aid from the wheel.

For the first time in days, Tree-ear grinned as he crushed the petal back into a fistful of clay. The second door had just blown open.

As usual, Min's work took far longer than he had predicted, and summer was merging with autumn before the pieces were ready. A dozen replicas had been fired in three separate batches, and the last firing yielded a pair of superb vases. Their delicate floral inlay work shone against the perfectly glazed background.

Under Min's instruction Tree-ear built a special *jiggeh* to wear on his back. As they worked, Min grumbled about the problem of transporting the vases, speaking more to himself than to Tree-ear.

105

Ajima came out to the yard with tea. She served them while Min continued his muttering.

'A straw container,' Ajima suggested. 'Such as those used to carry rice, only perhaps double thickness, lined with more straw and silk. The vases would be well protected.'

Min sipped his tea, then turned to Tree-ear. 'Do you know of one who could make such a container?'

So it was that Crane-man too came to work for Min. He and Min agreed on a price for the labour, and Crane-man began to weave the container under the eaves of Min's house.

Tree-ear would be leaving in a few days. The straw container had been completed. Sturdy, with double walls and an attached lid, it was exactly the size to take the vases and padding tightly packed.

Crane-man fussed about with his creation, making invisible adjustments to the straw. Ajima came out to see it; she and Tree-ear exchanged amused glances behind Crane-man's back.

'It is finished?' Ajima asked.

Crane-man stopped his poking and pinching and bowed to Ajima. 'It was an honour to be a part of this endeavour.'

Crane-man stood aside while Ajima lifted the lid of the

container and closed it again, fastening it with the straw bobble and braided loop. 'Fine work,' she said, nodding in quiet admiration.

Then she turned to Crane-man, her brow furrowed. 'Crane-man,' she said, 'I have a favour to ask of you.'

Crane-man stood up proudly on his one leg. 'Nothing that the honourable potter's wife could ask would be too much,' he answered.

Ajima bowed in turn. She glanced at Tree-ear and gestured at him with one hand. 'This one—I have grown accustomed to his assistance,' she said. 'A hundred little chores he does for me each day. It is a great help to me in my old age.'

Now it was Tree-ear's turn to bow, which he did in bafflement. What was in Ajima's mind?

'I would be most grateful, Crane-man, if you could come to the house and continue this work while Tree-ear is away,' she said. Then she hung her head a little and wrung her hands as if ashamed. 'I could not pay you. I hoped that perhaps my thanks in the form of a meal . . .'

Tree-ear felt an enormous wave of relief wash over him, but caught himself in time to show no emotion. It would not do to embarrass Crane-man. It had been his greatest worry—how Crane-man would eat while he was away.

Of course, his friend could always go back to rifling rubbish heaps and foraging in the woods. But Tree-ear had felt that it would be like abandoning him for Crane-man to go back to such scavenging. For days now he had been worrying over the problem—and Ajima had offered the answer unasked.

'Your offer of food is kindness itself,' Crane-man said. Tree-ear looked up in alarm. This was the phrase of polite refusal. What was Crane-man doing? 'I would be happy to come by from time to time,' he continued.

Ajima nodded soberly. Crane-man bent over and picked up his crutch, then bowed in farewell to her. 'I will see you back at the bridge, Tree-ear,' he said, and hopped away.

Tree-ear watched until Crane-man disappeared beyond the bend in the road, then turned to Ajima, a question in his eyes.

'Because he is proud, Tree-ear,' she said. 'He does not wish to be fed out of pity.'

Tree-ear kicked a small stone at his feet. Why was it that pride and foolishness were so often close companions?

Arms crossed and stance defiant, Tree-ear stood under the bridge and began to speak.

'I have a journey to make,' he said sternly. 'Over a

road unknown to me. A thousand things could go wrong. Do you not think I have enough to worry about?'

Crane-man looked up in surprise. Tree-ear had never before spoken to him in such anger.

'Are you thinking of me, my friend? Do not worry. I fed myself—and you, for that matter—for many years before you worked for Min. I can do so again. Do you think me so helpless now?'

'Not you!' Tree-ear shouted, flapping his arms in frustration like a giant bird. 'I am not talking of you! It is Min's wife I am thinking of! She is an old woman now— would you have her poor back ache from pulling weeds? And those long walks into the mountains, for mushrooms or berries—she should long ago have earned rest from such tasks! From her husband she gets no help at all. He thinks of nothing but his work!'

Tree-ear paused, his breath coming in gasps. He inhaled once, deeply, then spoke more quietly. 'Would you have me worry about her on my journey, friend? Why will you not help her? For in helping her you would be helping me.'

The shock ebbed from Crane-man's eyes now that Tree-ear was no longer shouting. He turned to face the river, his back to Tree-ear.

Tree-ear watched and waited. Crane-man's bad leg was shaking a little. In a moment, it shook harder. Now

109

Crane-man's whole body was trembling. Tree-ear stepped forward in concern. He had not meant to make his friend cry.

Tree-ear touched Crane-man on the shoulder. Crane-man waved one arm at him, still shaking. But he was not crying.

He was *laughing*. The silent laughter he had been suppressing burst out of him, and he laughed so hard that he dropped his crutch. Tree-ear picked it up and stood in silence, first puzzled, then annoyed when Crane-man's laughter showed no sign of stopping. If there was a joke, he had missed it.

'*Ai*, my friend,' Crane-man said at last, and drew in a long breath. A few last chuckles escaped him as he took the crutch from Tree-ear and leaned on it to sit on the ground. He looked up and jabbed the crutch at Tree-ear.

'A fine performance!' he exclaimed. 'I have never seen better.'

Tree-ear's mouth dropped open for an instant, but he recovered quickly. 'What do you mean, "performance"?' he demanded. 'You would question my sincerity?'

'No, little monkey. That I would never doubt.' He smiled, obviously still amused. 'If it means so much to you, I will go daily to the house of Min. There! Does that satisfy you?'

Tree-ear nodded grudgingly. The matter was settled, for he knew that Crane-man would keep his word. Tree-ear's speech had gained the desired result—although not exactly in the way that he had planned.

Two vases—not the ones chosen—were packed in the straw container as a test. They had been stuffed with silk and wrapped in more silk. Rice straw was layered between them and crammed into every pocket of space. Min, Ajima, and Crane-man all watched as Tree-ear picked up the container and hurled it with all his strength to the ground. Then he rolled it over and over and even kicked it a few times.

Min rushed forward and unhooked the straw bobble. He groped about inside, then nodded once in satisfaction. The vases were unbroken. 'Unpack it,' he ordered Tree-ear, then went inside to fetch the two selected vessels.

As soon as Min had left the yard, Crane-man stepped forward to examine the container. He, too, was satisfied; the woven straw had sustained no damage.

Repacked with its precious cargo, the container was lashed to the *jiggeh*. A sleeping mat was rolled tightly and tied to the bottom of the frame. On one side hung two pairs of sandals; on the other, a small gourd water dipper and a bag to be filled with rice cakes.

The *jiggeh* was ready. Tree-ear would leave in the morning.

*　　*　　*

Tree-ear and Crane-man skipped stones under the bridge in the twilight. Before the light was gone, Tree-ear reached into his waist pouch and slowly withdrew a small object. He handed it to Crane-man.

'A gift,' Tree-ear said. 'To remind you of your promise to go daily to the house of Min.' He did not want to say, *to remind you of me*.

Over the past month or so Tree-ear had filled his idle time by moulding clay. He kept a small ball in his waist pouch and experimented with it whenever he had the chance. After some time a shape began to form out of the clay; it was almost as if the clay was speaking to him, telling him what it wished to become.

A monkey. Similar to a water dropper Min had once made. Smaller than the palm of Tree-ear's hand, the monkey sat with its hands clasped before its round belly, looking content and well-fed. Tree-ear had inlaid two tiny spots for eyes and inscribed other details on its face, hands, fur. During the preparations for the final firing of the kiln, he had secreted the little monkey in a corner and managed to retrieve it afterwards without Min's notice. To Tree-ear's delight, it shared with the other vessels of that firing the fine grey-green glaze.

Tree-ear had concluded that moulding was not at all the same as throwing a pot on the wheel. Moulding lacked the same sense of wonder, and of course no perfectly symmetrical vessel could be made without the wheel. There were still times when the vision of the prunus vase he had once dreamed of making appeared in his mind's eye, as if mocking him.

In spite of this, Tree-ear found that he had enjoyed the incision work. He had spent hours on the details of the monkey's features, inscribing them with progressively finer points. This, at least, was the same process, whether on a moulded figure or a thrown pot. On seeing the monkey after it had been fired, Tree-ear felt a quiet thrill.

The monkey was hollow, like all the water droppers Min made. But as Crane-man had no need of such, Tree-ear had not added the water holes. It was simply a little figure, almost like a toy.

Crane-man examined the gift closely. He turned it over and around and stroked its smooth finish. He started to speak, but the sound of his voice was rusty and he shook his head instead.

He hobbled over to the basket where he kept his odds and ends, and brought forth a piece of twine. Still silent, he fixed the twine cleverly around the monkey, tied a firm knot, and slipped the loop around his belt. The monkey swung gaily at his waist. At last he spoke.

'I am honoured to wear it,' he said and bowed.

'The honour is mine,' Tree-ear responded.

Crane-man looked down and played with the monkey

113

in his fingers. 'I have no gift for you beyond words,' he said. 'I would tell you this. Of all the problems you may meet on your journey, it will be people who are the greatest danger. But it will also be people to whom you must turn if ever you are in need of aid. Remember this, my friend, and you will travel well.'

CHAPTER
10

With a sharp stone Tree-ear made another mark on the frame of the *jiggeh*. There were six marks, one for each day of his travels so far.

It was as Crane-man had predicted—one village, one day. Every morning Tree-ear had risen, washed in a stream, and eaten one of Ajima's rice cakes. He would walk until the sun was directly overhead, then find a shady spot to rest and drink from the gourd. As the sun moved on, so did he. Sometime during the late afternoon or early evening he would come upon a village and stop for the night.

The countryside custom of hospitality to travellers was a great comfort to him. He walked the main street of the village until someone—usually a child—enquired about his health and his journey. Tree-ear would accompany the child home, where the woman of the house always consented to let him sleep under the eaves. Most evenings a meal was provided as well; otherwise, Min had given Tree-ear a string of coins to buy food as needed. He kept them in his waist pouch along with his two flint stones and a ball of clay.

'I would think you will return with some of the coins unspent,' Min had said gruffly on the morning of departure. As he gave Tree-ear the money, Min had placed his hand for a brief moment on Tree-ear's shoulder. The touch so startled Tree-ear that he almost flinched. Min turned away without a word of farewell, but Tree-ear felt that touch on his shoulder for a long time after.

Ajima had given him a sack of food. Not only were there solid rice cakes, the best journey food, but also a surprise: a packet of *gokkam*—sweet dried persimmons. Tree-ear's eyes had widened in disbelief when he opened the packet during a break on the first day. He knew what they were, the sticky orange rounds; a kindly monk had given him some *gokkam* one autumn many years ago, in celebration of Buddha's birthday. That was the only time he had ever tasted it. This *gokkam* was even better, with each luscious piece reminding him of Ajima's care.

So smoothly had his journey progressed that Tree-ear had begun to relax a little. No mishap had befallen him or his cargo. The weather had been fine, the days still holding the heat of summer, the nights a cool relief. He slept with the *jiggeh* as a hard, high pillow, the discomfort almost welcome as a reminder of his duty.

Today, though, Tree-ear's trepidation had returned. The walking had been easy so far; after he had climbed over the mountain nearest Ch'ulp'o, the terrain had flattened out into endless rice fields. Now the land began to rise again. The next village was two days' walk away, over a spur of mountain. Tree-ear would be spending this night in the forest.

Once on the mountain path, Tree-ear began to feel more at ease. Though these mountains were unfamiliar to him, the trees were the same as at home—maple, oak, and wild plum giving way gradually to pines as he climbed higher. Tree-ear occupied his mind by identifying the birds he heard and the plants he saw. At one point, he even began to sing a little—but stopped abruptly when he realized he had been chanting Min's throwing song. *Stubborn old man*, Tree-ear thought, shaking his head.

The first edge of autumn had nudged its way into these woods; the leaves of some of the trees were rimmed in scarlet or gold. The air was fresh and cool as he trudged the shady path, and he began to feel foolish about his worries earlier in the day.

He had hoped to come across a hunter's lean-to or even a temple, but no such shelter appeared as the sun began to descend below the treetops. Tree-ear searched for a suitable place to spend the night. At a shallow stream running cheerfully across the path he drank from his little gourd. Wiping his hands on his tunic, he stood and looked around.

On the other side of the stream, not far from the path, two huge boulders stood. Tree-ear splashed across the stream and examined them. Between them was a little hollow. It was too small to sleep in, but Tree-ear liked the look of the huge rocks. If he settled there for the night, he would feel as though they were standing guard over him.

He struggled out of the *jiggeh* and set about collecting dead wood for a fire. He had nothing to cook, but a fire would cheer and warm him as night came on. After clearing a space, he made a circle of stones from the stream. Then he built a little pyramid of twigs leaning against one another in the centre of the circle. At the bottom of the pyramid went a bed of dried pine needles.

With a well-practised motion, Tree-ear struck the two flint stones together. A shower of sparks leapt to the pine needles. It took a few tries before a wisp of smoke curled up to signal the birth of a flame. Tree-ear shook his head in mock disgust. Crane-man nearly always started a fire on the first try.

Tree-ear sat leaning against one of the boulders. He put

the flint stones back into the pouch, then ate a rice cake from the bag, wrinkling his nose a little at the first bite. He had finished Ajima's rice cakes the day before, and the *gokkam* was long gone. These cakes had been purchased in the village, and they did not have the same taste or texture.

After his meal, Tree-ear took out the ball of clay. He began pinching, kneading, rolling—not making anything yet, just waiting for the clay to whisper an idea. Soon the smooth curved back of a turtle took shape. Forming its head was more difficult, and Tree-ear bent studiously over the work.

After a while he became aware that he was straining to see the clay by the light of the fire. He looked around; the sun was gone, its light lingering for a few moments longer. Tree-ear rose and untied the sleeping mat from the *jiggeh*. He unrolled it between the fire and the boulders and lay down on his stomach, his chin on his hands.

'*Two things a man never grows tired of watching,*' he heard Crane-man say in his mind. '*Fire and falling water. Always the same, yet always changing.*'

As the darkness grew, the fire began throwing odd shadows on the tree trunks around him. A sudden snap from the fire startled him, and he felt the uneasiness returning. *Time for sleep*, he told himself stoutly.

He closed his eyes, but only for a moment. The darkness

119

around him felt too big. Watching the fire for a while longer would lull him, he decided. It worked; between the warmth and the steady flickering of the flames, his eyelids grew heavy.

Tree-ear suddenly jerked wide awake; he had heard a noise that was not the noise of the fire. It was so slight that it almost wasn't a noise—a whisper of movement, a disturbance in the still night air. He raised himself up on one elbow, listening, searching in the dim light of the newly risen half-moon. Perhaps it was nothing.

Then he heard it again. This time there was no doubt. Something was moving through the forest not far from him. Something light-footed—an animal slipping weightlessly over the leaves . . .

Slowly, slowly, he picked up the *jiggeh*. He meant to squeeze it into the hollow between the two boulders but could not do so silently. The branches of the *jiggeh* scraped against the granite. Tree-ear froze, holding his breath.

This would never do. He had to work quickly, or the creature, whatever it was, would be upon him before he knew it. He shoved the *jiggeh* into the opening, put his back to it, and wiggled in himself. There was not enough room; he crouched, hunched over with his chin on his knees, and waited, his heart nearly bursting through his chest.

Would the beast stay away from the fire? It was dying

now, not much more than a bed of coals. Tree-ear cursed himself for not having put more wood nearby.

The sound was coming closer; he could hear the rustle of leaves clearly off to his left. On the ground before him was a stick. It was only a twig, but Tree-ear reached for it anyway. He stripped the leaves from it and gripped it tightly. Perhaps, he thought wildly, he could blind the beast as it clawed at him, trying to drag him from between the rocks . . .

How long would he have to wait? The moments crawled by. Then without further warning, the creature came into view.

It was a fox!

Tree-ear felt his pulse pounding in his throat. His thoughts seemed to be running a desperate race with each other. Against a fox he was defenceless. The fox would stare at him, looking deep into his eyes, bewitching him until he rose to follow it to its lair. He would never see Crane-man or Ajima again. The vases would remain hidden between the rocks for eternity. There would be nothing left of him but a pile of gnawed bones . . .

The fox turned its head. For an instant the firelight gleamed in its eyes. *Don't look!* Tree-ear shouted to himself. *Don't look at its eyes—it's your only chance!* And he squeezed his eyes shut to block out the fox's evil stare.

How long he waited he did not know. He opened his

eyes after what seemed a lifetime. Had he been bewitched despite his efforts? Was he in the fox's lair, conscious for one last moment before a painful, bloody death?

Tree-ear blinked to clear his vision. The fox was gone. He was still wedged into the opening between the rocks, his muscles aching with cramp. He dared not move; it was probably just another of the fox's tricks. If he were to emerge from shelter, the fox would be there, waiting for him. No, he would have to remain there, alert for any trap the devilish creature might spring . . .

The sound of crying birds awoke him. For a moment Tree-ear did not know where he was. He shifted slightly and a corner of the *jiggeh*'s frame jabbed him rudely in the back.

Sunlight streamed gloriously through the trees. It was morning.

Could it be? He had fallen asleep! He had slept for who knew how long, with a fox nearby—and he had survived!

Tree-ear laughed out loud, and the sound of his laughter reminded him of his friend. *We are afraid of the things we do not know—just because we do not know them*, Tree-ear thought, pleased with himself. He must remember the idea; Crane-man would be interested in discussing it. And he wiggled out of the crevice, grimacing ruefully at the tight knots in what seemed like every one of his muscles.

* * *

A day's walk beyond the next village lay the city of Puyo. Although Tree-ear was determined to go straight to Songdo without delay, Crane-man had counselled him to make one stop—at a place called the 'Rock of the Falling Flowers' in Puyo.

'It is an old, old story,' Crane-man had said. And Tree-ear had settled down on his sleeping mat, wriggling around for the most comfortable position.

'You know that our little land has suffered many invasions,' Crane-man began. 'The powers that surround us—China, Japan, the Mongols—have never left us in peace for long. This is the story of one such invasion.

'It was the T'ang Chinese this time, all of five hundred years ago. Puyo was then the capital of the Paekche kingdom—one of the Three Kingdoms that shared the land. The T'ang, allied with the Silla kingdom, swept down from the north and pushed their way into Puyo. Most of the king's army having been called away to fight the war, there were only a handful of personal guards to defend him. The king received warning, but it was too late.

'As he and all his courtiers fled the palace, the T'ang were snapping at their heels. The king and his party were forced to retreat to the very highest point of Puyo—a cliff overlooking the Kum River. There was no escape. Bravely, the king's guards placed themselves a little way down the path between the enemy and their sovereign. They were overrun in moments.

'All of the king's concubines and ladies-in-waiting crowded around him, determined to protect him to the last. The women knew well that the T'ang would not kill them; no, they would be taken prisoner, probably to be tortured. Their terror can hardly be imagined.'

Crane-man paused and sipped at his tea. Tree-ear was no longer lying down; he had risen to his knees in the excitement of the story. 'Is that all?' he demanded.

'Patience, monkey. The best is yet to come.' Crane-man stared into the fire for a moment. 'The T'ang army charged up the hill. All at once, as if all their minds had become one, the women began jumping off the cliff. Every one of them preferred death to becoming a prisoner.

'Can you see it, my friend? The women jumping one after another from the cliff, their beautiful silk dresses billowing in the air—pink, red, green, blue . . . indeed, like flowers falling.'

Tree-ear gasped, his eyes round. What courage it must have taken!

'The T'ang were victorious that day, but the women's efforts were not in vain, for they have since been an inspiration to all who have need of courage. Their memory will live for a thousand years, I am sure of it.'

Crane-man reached out with his crutch and poked the

dying embers of the fire. Tree-ear saw sparks flare up and fall again . . . like tiny flowers.

'Go climb the Rock of the Falling Flowers when you reach Puyo, my friend,' Crane-man had said. 'But remember that leaping into death is not the only way to show true courage.'

Now Puyo lay just ahead. Tree-ear strode eagerly down the road. He would visit the rock, and when he returned home, he would tell Crane-man everything he had seen.

The villages along Tree-ear's route thus far were much like Ch'ulp'o. They were not seaside villages, and they were inhabited by farmers rather than potters, but they had the same feel as Ch'ulp'o: small thatched houses gathered in clusters along a single main road, the grand home of a government official set apart from the rest, a temple some-where nearby, people working hard for a meagre living. Everyone had been kind and respectful, going about their business as he went about his.

But Puyo! Tree-ear entered the city gates and stopped in midstep. How crowded it was! People, oxen, and carts jostled one another in the narrow streets; the houses were so close together that Tree-ear wondered how their residents could breathe. Behind him he heard shouts of impatience, as people tried to push past him. He moved on, swept along by the river of traffic.

On both sides of the street shop stalls were open. Their owners shouted, plying their wares; the customers shouted, bargaining for the best prices. Never had Tree-ear seen so many goods displayed—or heard so much noise! How could the people of Puyo possibly hear themselves think?

There were stalls that sold food and drink already prepared, and stalls that sold vegetables and fish for cooking at home. One stall sold nothing but sweets. There were bolts of fine silk, trays of gemstones, wooden toys. All manner of household goods could be had, baskets and straw sleeping mats and wooden chests.

And pottery. Tree-ear stopped abruptly in front of one stall. It was stacked with small mountains of pottery—not celadon work, but the very dark brown stoneware known as *onggi*, for storing food.

The *onggi* seller's stall displayed every size of vessel—from tiny sauce dishes to *kimchee* jars big enough for a man to stand hidden within. The wares were stacked in tall towers that seemed to tilt precariously. But Tree-ear smiled, knowing they were steadier than they looked. He had learned well how to stack similar-sized vessels into a tower that could touch the sky if need be and never topple.

Tree-ear was just about to move on when he spotted a shelf at the back of the stall. His mouth dropped open in amazement.

126

Just three objects stood on this shelf, three identical celadon wine bowls—*inlaid with chrysanthemums*.

The owner noticed Tree-ear's interest. 'Boy, tell your master—the latest style, those bowls are. The design is a favourite of the king himself! I dare not tell you what I paid for them . . . only a customer of impeccable taste could afford such an item. Is your master such a one?'

Tree-ear did not mean to be rude, but he could not speak. He merely bowed his head to the man and stepped away from the stall, feeling a little dizzy.

Kang's designs—already seen and admired and replicated for sale on the streets of Puyo.

Tree-ear began to walk faster, shouldering his way through the crowds. The sooner the better for Min's work to reach Songdo.

CHAPTER

11

The path to the Rock of the Falling Flowers was steep, and Tree-ear leaned forward, sometimes on all fours, as he climbed. Just before he reached the top, he stopped by the side of the path and took the *jiggeh* off his back. He drank from the gourd and poured a little water on his hands to splash on his sweaty face.

Thus refreshed, he felt ready to give his full attention to the sight of the rock. He walked the last incline holding the *jiggeh* awkwardly in front of him and set it down once he reached the broad plateau at the top.

It was as if he stood alone on top of the world. He gazed around, this way and that, hardly knowing where to look first. Before him to the north the cliff fell away sharply to the Kum River, a broad stroke of silver ribboning its way through the hills and plains. Behind him was the

128

path he had climbed, with the city of Puyo below. How small it looked now! Tree-ear shaded his eyes from the sun as it began to set, wondering if that smudge on the horizon might be the sea. Surely this cliff was high enough to see all the way there.

Crane-man's words came to life—the king standing where Tree-ear stood now, surrounded by the palace women . . . the enemy scrambling up the path he had just followed . . . the cries of the women—their terror and then their sudden act of bravery, their coloured dresses like the petals of thousands of flowers.

'You know the story, eh?' The voice at his side startled Tree-ear; he felt his heart leap and run. He had not heard the man come up the path, but there he stood, poorly dressed and oddly pale, as if he had been ill for a long time or never went outdoors when the sun shone.

Tree-ear cleared his throat. 'Greetings, sir. Have you eaten well today?'

'Not today, not for a few days now,' came the impolite answer. The man smiled, but Tree-ear did not like his smile. There was something unpleasant behind it. Although he would have preferred to stay at the rock a while longer, he decided to descend rather than remain in unwanted company.

Tree-ear turned and picked up his *jiggeh*, preparing to hoist it to his back.

'Let me help you with that,' the man said, moving forward. 'A fine load of rice indeed!'

Tree-ear stepped back, trying to quell his alarm. His cargo was far more precious than rice. 'Your offer is kind, good sir, but I have no need of help.'

The man's smile turned into a leer. 'Now, there's a rude boy—my help is no good to you?' And he reached out with one arm to grab the *jiggeh*.

Tree-ear jerked it away from him. He stumbled, coming dangerously near the edge of the cliff. The man snarled, menacing and ugly, and advanced a few steps. He seized the sides of the straw container with both hands and pulled.

In the last moments everything had come together in Tree-ear's mind. The man's pallor . . . his rudeness . . . his coming upon Tree-ear in such a deserted place. He was one of the dreaded *toduk-non*, the bandits who hid throughout the countryside and on the outskirts of cities, emerging only to rob weary travellers. Tree-ear held on to the wooden frame of the *jiggeh* with all his might.

The robber pulled and jerked; Crane-man's solid straw work held. At one point the man released one hand, cursing—the straw had cut into his palm. Tree-ear's hands were toughened by calluses from axe and spade, his arms strengthened by endless work; he gave not a single step of ground to the robber.

130

Be careful! A scream of warning sounded in Tree-ear's head. *You are pulling so hard. If he lets go suddenly, you will fall! Move, move now, so your back is not to the cliff edge!*

Tree-ear shifted his feet and began edging sideways. Still the robber pulled, now shouting curses and threats with every breath. Soon Tree-ear's back was to the path. His hands and arms felt like iron—they would never break, he would never let go. The robber was weakening, he could feel it . . .

Tree-ear stared into the robber's face; hatred would give him more strength. And it did, too; silently he swore to himself that this dog of a man would never win the *jiggeh* with its priceless contents.

The man stared back at him, his face contorted in an evil grimace. But suddenly he laughed and released the container. Tree-ear collapsed backwards—into the arms of another man who had stolen up the path behind him.

A second robber.

Against two, Tree-ear could do nothing. The second man pinned his arms back while the first strode forward and wrenched the *jiggeh* away. Tree-ear kicked and struggled. His head crashed into the chin of his captor, who swore in pain; the other robber reached out and slapped Tree-ear's face viciously.

'Stop your struggle, worthless one,' he said. 'We mean

only to rob you, but it would not be past us to harm you if you prove too much trouble.'

While his companion kept Tree-ear pinioned, the first robber quickly opened the straw container. He threw aside the packing of straw and silk, growing angrier with each handful.

'Not rice! What is it you are carrying, idiot-boy?' At last, he drew out the first of the vases and his face grew purple with fury.

'Useless!' he screamed, gripping the mouth of the vase with one hand and waving it about. Tree-ear caught his breath with fear.

'We might sell it,' said the second robber more calmly.

'Have you no eyes in your head?' his companion shouted back. 'Look at it—can't you see, this could only be a gift for the palace! Nobody would dare buy it from us!'

'Keep looking. Perhaps there is something more.'

The robber set the first vase down on the ground and returned to his search of the container. With more muttered curses, he pulled out the second vessel and threw a final handful of straw on the ground.

'Nothing!' he screamed. 'All the way up this hill—and nothing!'

His companion had shifted his grip and now had one arm across Tree-ear's throat, throttling him so he could

132

barely breathe. With his other hand he pawed roughly at Tree-ear's waist pouch.

'Eh—here is something to cheer you up!' He held the pouch in his free hand and emptied the contents onto the ground. The flint stones and the little clay turtle fell out, followed by the string of coins.

'Something, anyway,' grumbled the first robber, scooping up the coins. He kicked the *jiggeh* out of his way and headed down the path. 'Come—we've wasted enough time here.'

Tree-ear breathed a silent prayer of thanks. *Take the money—take anything. Just leave the vases alone . . .*

The second robber laughed. 'Wait,' he said. 'Come hold this donkey for a moment.'

The first robber retraced his steps. 'What is it?' he asked impatiently, grabbing Tree-ear by the arms from behind.

'A little fun, as long as we're up here.'

The robber picked up one of the vases. He stepped to the edge of the cliff—and flung it into the air. Peering over the edge, he put his hand to his ear in a pose of listening. After an agony of silence, the crash of pottery was heard on the rocks far below.

The second robber laughed again. 'One more!' he said in a jovial voice.

'No!' Tree-ear screamed, an inhuman screech of utter

133

desperation. The robber holding him lifted him off his feet and slammed him to the ground so hard that his breath left him.

And Tree-ear could only watch as the second vase sailed through the air. With a yelp like a wounded dog, he put his hands over his ears so he would not hear the crash.

Tree-ear rolled onto his side and vomited. He retched again and again, until his stomach felt as empty as his spirit. Shakily, he rose to his feet and bent over double, his hands on his knees.

Failure. The most dishonourable failure. He had been unable to keep the vases safe; Puyo was not even halfway to Songdo. If he had reached his destination and the work had been rejected by the court, at least he would have done his part.

He raised his head slowly and stared at the edge of the cliff. He thought of returning to Min with this news, and his whole body shuddered. Nothing could be worse. He straightened up and took a few steps towards the edge.

What would it be like? To leap off and sail through the air as those women had—like flying, like a bird, so free. And time would feel different. Those few moments would feel like hours, surely . . .

But just then he heard Crane-man's voice so clearly that he turned in surprise. '*Leaping into death is not the only way to show true courage.*' No one was there, of course. Tree-ear stepped back from the edge, ashamed. He knew it was true; it would take far more courage to face Min. He thought of his promise to Ajima, and besides, Crane-man was waiting for him. It was his duty to return.

He picked up his waist pouch and put the flint stones and the turtle back inside. Then he untied the few items from the *jiggeh*. There was one pair of sandals; he had donned the other spare pair the day before. The food bag still held a few rice cakes, but Tree-ear felt that he would never be able to eat again.

He tucked the pouch back under his tunic and slung the sandals, the food bag and the drinking gourd over one shoulder. Then he stood for a few moments staring at nothing. Gradually, the empty straw container came into focus before him. With a sudden cry of fury, Tree-ear picked up the *jiggeh* and threw it, container and all, over the edge of the cliff. He watched its descent; it did not fall cleanly to the water but bounced several times off the rocks on its way down.

Tree-ear turned and began to run. He ran blindly down the mountain path, heedless of the rocks and shrubs. Several times he fell but was on his feet again in the next breath, stumbling, tripping, skidding in a headlong descent. When at last he reached the point where the path levelled out, he fell hard onto his face, the dirt mixing with his tears. His teeth cut into his top lip and he spat blood. The pain was welcome; he deserved far worse.

Tree-ear sat up and wiped his face with the edge of his tunic, hearing nothing but the sound of his own panting and the rushing river nearby. Suddenly, a last flicker of hope flared within him. The second vase—he had not heard the crash. Perhaps it had fallen into the water, perhaps it was still unbroken . . .

Tree-ear made his way around the base of the cliff to the river. Boulders blocked the way to a narrow strip of sand, with more rocks beyond. He looked up the sheer face of the cliff as it rose far above him and tried to guess where the vases might have fallen. Then he began scrambling over the boulders.

Thorny shrubs grew among the rocks. Sometimes they massed into a wall so thick that he had to scramble down to the water's edge and wade to make further progress. If the vases had fallen among those shrubs, he would never be able to find them.

That small mass on the sand up ahead, not as dark as the rocks—could that be a vase? Tree-ear made his awkward way over the stony ground, barking his shin once but hardly feeling the pain in his eagerness.

No. A pile of pebbles.

For a long time, he made his way back and forth between

the cliff and the river, up and down over the rocks and sand. He had nearly given up hope when he came upon a little mound of shards.

They would never have been noticed by a casual passerby; so thoroughly smashed was the vessel that the fragments were no bigger than pebbles. Tree-ear crouched and touched them gingerly. *The first vase*, he hoped with all his might.

He stood and looked around. The thief had thrown both vases from the same spot on the cliff; the other one should be somewhere nearby. At the river's edge, Tree-ear saw something on the sand. He approached it slowly, telling himself it was probably another pile of pebbles or a piece of driftwood . . .

It was the second vase. The force of its fall had driven it into the sand—in a hundred pieces.

Tree-ear dropped to his knees. *Fool*, he thought bitterly. *Fool, to hope that it could have survived such a fall.*

The second vase, its fall cushioned however slightly by the sand, had broken into bigger pieces. The largest shard was the size of his palm. Tree-ear picked up this piece and swished it through the water to rinse off the sand.

Across one side of the shard ran a shallow groove, evidence of the vase's melon shape. Part of an inlaid peony blossom with its stem and leaves twined along the groove. And the glaze still shone clear and pure, untouched by the violence that had just been done it.

A sharp edge of the shard bit into Tree-ear's palm. The pain was an echo—he remembered now. It was when he had thrown the shard from the first batch of ruined vases into the river in Ch'ulp'o. How long ago it seemed!

Suddenly, Tree-ear raised his head. He stood up and squared his shoulders, still clutching the piece of pottery. He laid the shard carefully on a flat stone. He took the clay turtle from his waist pouch and squeezed it back into a ball. Next he rolled the clay between his palms until it formed a long snake. Picking up the shard again, he pinched the snake all the way around the sharp edge to protect it.

Tree-ear removed the flint stones from his waist pouch; they might scratch the shard. He tied them into one corner of his tunic, then put the clay-bound shard into the pouch. Holding the pouch clear of the boulders with one hand, he climbed back to the path.

His every movement was quick with purpose; to hesitate was to doubt. He had made up his mind: he would journey on to Songdo and show the emissary the single shard.

Chapter

12

The next several days passed in a steady blur. Tree-ear walked and walked. The sun shone; he walked. Rain poured; he walked. From sunrise until dark he walked without stopping, drinking from the gourd along the way.

If dark found him near a village, he slept outside a house and accepted whatever was offered in the way of food. If there was no village, he slept in a ditch by the side of the road or under a tree in the forest. He ate perhaps once every two days, feeling no need of food but knowing that without it he could not complete the journey.

Only once did he pause. A low range of mountains made a bowl of a valley cut through by a beautiful river. After crossing the valley, Tree-ear stopped on a peak at the far side and looked back. He knew that the scene must be even lovelier than it now looked to him, viewed as it was through a fog of exhaustion that blurred his senses and his mind. Perhaps on the way back he would appreciate it more.

Three days' walk north of this valley brought him to Songdo.

Songdo was like Puyo, only more so—more people, more buildings, more traffic. The palace was in the centre of the city, towering over all other structures.

Tree-ear did not stop walking. Every step brought him closer to the palace. Once he shuffled sideways to avoid a woman with a toddler tied to her back. The toddler was crying over some unknown disappointment, and the sound of his cries drew Tree-ear's attention. He watched as the mother comforted the child by rhythmically bouncing up and down and crooning to him.

For just a moment Tree-ear was distracted. He had been such a child once, right here in Songdo. He had lived here with his parents—a father and a mother. Perhaps his mother had comforted him in the same way when he had cried. Perhaps somewhere, in one of the temples, there was a monk who knew about his parents, who remembered sending him to Ch'ulp'o.

Tree-ear sighed and looked back out on the street. The

noise of the traffic seemed to press in on his ears, on his very body. Everywhere there were people hurrying about. There must be dozens of temples in the mountains surrounding Songdo; even if Tree-ear could find that monk, it was likely that he would no longer remember. He might even be dead by now.

It was useless to wonder. Tree-ear turned his mind back to his task.

Late in the afternoon Tree-ear made his steady way through the crowds and found the main gate of the palace. Two soldiers stood guard there.

He spoke firmly. 'I have an appointment with the royal emissary for pottery ware,' he said, for that was Emissary Kim's full title. He made a dignified bow.

The guards looked at Tree-ear, then at each other. Tree-ear could read their thoughts—*This scrawny scarecrow of a child claims a royal appointment?* But he felt no trembling now; his calm did not even surprise him. He was expected. He had the right to be there.

His manner must have said as much, for one of the guards vanished beyond the gate. He was gone long enough for the other guard to shift impatiently, but Tree-ear did not budge. He stood proudly, his eyes never leaving the gate.

At last the guard returned, followed by another man. It

was not Emissary Kim, but he was garbed in a similar robe, wearing a different hat—some kind of official of lower rank than Kim. He, too, looked sceptically at Tree-ear.

'Yes?' he enquired, his politeness edged with impatience.

Tree-ear bowed again. 'I have an appointment with Emissary Kim. I am here on behalf of Potter Min from Ch'ulp'o.'

The official raised his eyebrows slightly. 'Yes, all right. Where is the work? I will take it to Emissary Kim, and you may return for his answer in a few days.'

Tree-ear paused before he spoke. 'I do not wish to displease the honourable gentleman, but I will not show what I have brought to anyone but the emissary.' He drew in a silent breath to quell the small nudge of anxiety that was rising within him; so far he had not been forced to lie.

The official looked annoyed. 'Emissary Kim is a very busy man. I do not wish to disturb him when he could view the work at his convenience.'

'Then I will wait for his convenience,' said Tree-ear. He looked directly at the man. 'Emissary Kim has specifically requested that Potter Min's work be brought to him. I do not wish him to be disappointed.'

His message was clear to the official. 'I understand,' the man said crossly, 'but surely you do not expect to see him without showing him the work. Where is it?'

'I will discuss its whereabouts with no one but the emissary.'

The official muttered under his breath and finally seemed to make up his mind. He nodded to the guards. The gate swung open and Tree-ear stepped inside the royal courtyard.

Inside the gate lay another small city. Buildings lined the walls and across a wide stretch of open courtyard Tree-ear could see the grandest of them all—the palace proper. Tree-ear nearly tripped as he walked with his neck craned and his eyes wide; he had never before seen a building more than one storey high.

And wonder of wonders, the palace had celadon roof tiles.

Tree-ear stopped walking. He had heard of these roof tiles. Years ago, before his time, potters in Ch'ulp'o had been engaged in the enormous task of making those very tiles. 'Wasters', the rejects, could still be found around the kiln site. How Tree-ear wished he could somehow climb the walls and examine the tiles more closely! Even from where he stood he could make out their intricate relief work.

All sorts of people went about their business—tradesmen and soldiers and officials and many monks. Reluctantly, Tree-ear turned his attention away from the tiles and caught up with his escort. The official led the way deeper into the palace grounds. He stopped at last before a building against the outer wall and gestured for Tree-ear to wait outside.

After a few moments the official returned and beckoned Tree-ear. Tree-ear walked through an entryway into a small room—small, but lovely. Shelves along one wall held celadon vessels; Tree-ear could see at a glance that each piece was of the highest quality. The official who had led him in moved to stand at one side of the door in the stance of an assistant.

Emissary Kim sat at a low wooden table. He was writing rapidly on a scroll, the brush racing across the paper, leaving behind a trail of perfectly formed characters. Tree-ear could not read, but he could see the skill of Kim's calligraphy.

Kim wiped the brush carefully on the inkstone. He picked up the scroll and carried it to a shelf where it would dry. Then he returned to the table and sat again. He folded his arms and looked at Tree-ear.

Tree-ear bowed low. As he bent down, his courage suddenly fled, leaving his knees as weak as reeds. *I must be hungry*, he thought as he straightened his body, incredulous that he could think of such a thing at such a moment.

'You are here from Ch'ulp'o. From Potter Min,' the emissary stated.

'Yes, honourable sir.'

The emissary waited. 'Well?' he said. 'Where is the work?'

Tree-ear swallowed hard. 'Sir, on my way here, I was set upon by robbers. They—they destroyed my master's work—'

The assistant stepped forward in anger. 'How dare you, brazen fool! How dare you demand an audience of the emissary with nothing to show him!' He reached to grab Tree-ear's arm and yank him out of the door.

The weakness in Tree-ear's knees surged through his whole body now. The assistant was right. He had been a fool. First a failure, now a fool . . .

But the emissary had risen to his feet and gestured at his aide, who stepped back, chastened.

'I am greatly disappointed,' Emissary Kim said. 'I have so looked forward to seeing Potter Min's work again.'

Tree-ear hung his head. 'Humblest apologies to the honourable emissary,' he mumbled. Slowly, he took the shard from his waist pouch. He drew in a deep breath and looked down at the shard before he spoke.

How odd it looked, with its rough frame of clay. But the inlay work was still delicate and clear, the glaze still fine and pure. Seeing it gave Tree-ear a last pulse of courage.

'It is but a fragment, Honourable Emissary. And yet, I

believe that it shows all of my master's skill.' And he held it out before him in cupped hands.

The emissary looked surprised but accepted the offering. He inspected it carefully. He even took off the crude wrapping of clay and peered at the edges of the shard.

Then Emissary Kim sat down at his table again. He chose one of the scrolls before him, took up his brush, and began writing.

Tree-ear stood with his head bowed to hide tears of shame. Obviously, the emissary had already moved on to other business, but it would be rude for Tree-ear to leave before he had been dismissed. He wondered if he should take back the shard, which the emissary had placed carefully on the table. Amid his despair, Tree-ear still felt grateful—grateful that the emissary had not laughed in his face for the stupidity of travelling all that way with only a single shard to show.

At his side he heard the assistant gasp in surprise. The emissary had beckoned the man and was showing him the scroll.

'Go. See that it is done,' said the emissary.

'Master—' The assistant hesitated. 'How is it that a commission can be awarded without seeing the work?' The man's courteous words could not mask the disapproval in his voice.

'I understand your scepticism,' the emissary answered

patiently. 'But I have seen this man's work, in Ch'ulp'o and again here.' He bent and picked up the shard from the table.

'Do you see this? "Radiance of jade and clarity of water"—that is what is said about the finest celadon glaze. It is said of very few pieces.' He paused for a moment and held the shard up before him. 'I say it of this one. And the inlay work . . . remarkable.' His voice faded for a moment as he gazed in obvious admiration at the shard. Then he handed the scroll to the assistant. 'Now, go and do as I bid you.'

The assistant bowed abruptly and left. Emissary Kim looked at Tree-ear. There was kindness in his eyes—like Crane-man's, like Ajima's.

'I have written orders for him to secure your passage back to Ch'ulp'o by sea,' he said. 'You will go and deliver a message to your master for me. I am assigning him a commission. Tell me, have you worked for Potter Min long?'

Tree-ear was reeling from the man's words, spoken in such a calm, ordinary voice. Through a haze of disbelief and confusion, he heard himself answer. 'A year and a half, honourable sir.'

'Good. Then perhaps you can tell me—for your master to do his best work, how many pieces per year might I expect from him?'

Concentrating on the answer to the emissary's question helped steady Tree-ear. 'I think ten. Not fewer, but not many more . . .' He looked up and spoke with quiet pride. 'My master works slowly.'

The emissary nodded solemnly. 'As well he should.' He bowed his head to Tree-ear. 'If you have need of shelter here in Songdo, my assistant will see to it that you are housed and fed until the boat sails. Your coming is greatly appreciated.'

Tree-ear wanted to laugh, to cry, to fling his arms around the emissary and dance wildly around the room. Instead, he bowed all the way to the ground. He could not speak but prayed that the emissary understood his silent thanks.

There were some things that could not be moulded into words.

CHAPTER
13

The journey by sea was much faster than the journey across land. After the first day—when he had been sick, both from excitement and from the rolling of the deck—Tree-ear enjoyed watching the sea in all its changes. And the sky looked different, much larger than it looked over land. Still, his main feeling during the journey was one of tingling impatience.

At last, the boat drew near Ch'ulp'o, and Tree-ear leaned eagerly over the side. How familiar the village looked, even from this strange new angle! In his eagerness, Tree-ear had to stop himself from leaping into the sea when the boat was still far from shore. The final stretch of the trip—from deep water to the beach in a small rowing boat—seemed to take the longest of all.

From the landing beach Tree-ear hurried towards the

village. He had decided to go to Min first, to deliver the message about the commission, and then return to the bridge to tell Crane-man the news.

No one answered his call at the front of the house, so Tree-ear walked around to the back. Ajima was in the vegetable patch, crouched over with her back to him.

He cleared his throat. 'Ajima?'

She whirled around so quickly that for a moment he feared she would fall over. 'Tree-ear!' she exclaimed, her face breaking into the thousand wrinkles of her smile. 'You are safely returned!'

'Yes, Ajima.'

The day was chilly, autumn fully arrived, but her welcome swept over Tree-ear like a warm breeze. He bowed and could not keep himself from smiling in return. 'Is the master home?'

'He is at the draining site—' She hesitated as if making a decision, then spoke again. 'You have news for him?'

Tree-ear felt his smile grow broader. 'Yes, Ajima.' He bowed again to her and scampered through the yard towards the stream.

Tree-ear slowed to a walk as he neared the clearing. He balled his fists tightly to contain his excitement.

'Master Potter?' he called.

Min was stirring the clay in the drainage bed. He put

the paddle down and wiped his hands on a rag. 'You are back,' he said simply.

Tree-ear bowed. 'I saw the royal emissary,' he said, trying to keep his voice from sounding too important. 'He has assigned you a commission.'

Min closed his eyes and drew in a long, long breath. He let out the air in a sigh that was almost a whistle and opened his eyes. For a moment he stared off into the distance over Tree-ear's shoulder, then walked over to a boulder by the stream and sat down. He indicated another boulder at his side.

Tree-ear sat down, disappointed that Min was so subdued. Tree-ear's own heart was still pounding so hard that he could feel his pulse in his throat. He glanced surreptitiously at the potter's face. Why did Min look so solemn? Was this not the news he had awaited nearly all his life? Tree-ear shrugged in his mind; it was what he should have expected from the potter.

Min leaned forward, started to speak, then stopped and shook his head. 'I am sorry, Tree-ear,' he said at last. 'Your friend from under the bridge—'

Tree-ear froze. *Crane-man*.

'He was up on the bridge a few days ago. A farmer tried to cross with too great a load on his cart. The wood of the bridge railing was rotten. Your friend was bumped and jostled, and the railing broke.'

Tree-ear closed his eyes. He wanted Min to stop talking.

Min leaned forward and put his hand on Tree-ear's shoulder. 'The water was so cold . . . your friend was old. The shock was too great for his heart.'

Tree-ear felt very strange. It was as if he had stepped out of his body and was watching himself listen to Min. This other, detached Tree-ear noticed that Min's eyes were soft, his face gentle. It was the first time Tree-ear had ever seen him so.

Min was still speaking. 'I am told that it was very sudden, Tree-ear. Your friend did not suffer.' He reached into his waist pouch and drew forth a small object. 'When they pulled him from the river, he was clutching this in his hand.'

It was the little ceramic monkey, still on its crude string. Min held it forth, but Tree-ear could not move to take it.

Tree-ear heard Ajima's voice then. She seemed to appear out of thin air at his side. Or had she been there the whole time? The sounds and sights around him were wavering, as if seen and heard through water. 'Tree-ear, you will stay with us tonight,' she said.

With his thoughts still outside his body, Tree-ear watched himself stand and allow Ajima to lead him back to the house.

Min called after them. 'It is fine work, Tree-ear,' he said.

The words came to Tree-ear as if from a great distance;

his ears could not be trusted. Perhaps he had only imagined them.

He and Ajima stepped over the threshold. The part of Tree-ear's mind that was still working marvelled at this; he had never been inside the house before. He caught glimpses of Min's work—a fine teapot on a shelf, an inscribed jar that held cooking tools. The rooms seemed neat and spare, but not cold with tidiness.

Ajima showed him to a small narrow room with a sleeping mat already unrolled, then left him alone. Tree-ear lay down on the mat. He closed his eyes to the light and his mind to what he had just heard, and fell into a deep dark hole of sleep.

The next morning Tree-ear rose long before the temple bell. He left the silent house and walked to the stream, where he stood staring at the motion of the current. Then he bent and picked up a flat stone, but threw it so carelessly that it did not skip at all. It dropped into the water with a loud *plunk*.

Tree-ear threw a second rock, then a third. Suddenly, he was hurling a barrage of rocks into the water, one after the other, harder and harder, until the water roiled and foamed beneath the rain of rocks. In a senseless frenzy Tree-ear threw leaves and sticks and clods of dirt—whatever he could get his hands on.

Finally, he had no breath left. He bent over, clutching his stomach and panting, then knelt in the mud of the stream bank and watched the troubled water subside.

If he hadn't volunteered to take Min's work to Songdo, what then? He might have been there; he could have helped . . .

The current carried a drifting leaf into a little eddy. Tree-ear's thoughts swirled back to the day that he had given his friend the gift. He recalled Crane-man's solemn pleasure, and how he had immediately sought a piece of twine to keep the monkey near him always. Crane-man had never even hinted that Tree-ear should not make the journey. He had been proud of Tree-ear's courage.

Memories layered themselves in Tree-ear's mind: Crane-man's willingness to discuss things with him . . . the stories he told, the mountain secrets he shared, his reading of the world around them . . . the way he loved a joke, even at the expense of himself or his bad leg.

Another recollection broke through his thoughts, like a fish breaking the surface of water. 'Wherever you are on your journey, Crane-man,' Tree-ear whispered, 'I hope you are travelling on two good legs.'

The tears came then.

The sound of the temple bell cut through Tree-ear's muffled sobs. He rose shakily, washed his face in the stream, and walked slowly back to the house. Min was waiting for him in the yard—with the cart and the axe.

Wood today, Tree-ear sighed to himself. Nothing had changed. Everything was as it had been before his journey.

No. Not the same at all. Crane-man was gone. Tree-ear shivered. How would he endure the coming winter, alone in the dank vegetable pit?

Min handed him the axe. 'Large logs,' he barked. 'At minimum, the girth of a man's body.'

Tree-ear frowned. Why so large? True, such logs could be split to fit through the kiln openings, but this required extra work.

'What's the matter with you, boy? Do you not understand that I have been assigned a royal commission? Do you not realize how much work it will be?'

Tree-ear hung his head as Min's scolding continued. 'How am I to do it all myself? How are you to help me if you do not have a wheel of your own? And how is the wheel to be made if you do not fetch logs of considerable size? Go!' Min gestured impatiently towards the mountains.

Tree-ear had already turned to leave when the full import of Min's words reached his understanding. *A wheel of your own?*

Min was going to teach him to throw pots! Tree-ear glanced back over his shoulder, a foolishly wide grin on his face. But Min had already gone back inside, and it was Ajima who waved to him from the yard, beckoning him to return for a lunch bowl. 'Be home in time for supper,' she said as she handed it to him.

It was his second great surprise in as many moments. *Home*, Ajima had said. Tree-ear looked at her, puzzled. Ajima nodded solemnly.

'Tree-ear, if you would live with us from now on, I would ask a favour of you.'

'Anything, Ajima.' Tree-ear bowed, feeling a little dizzy.

'We would like to give you a new name. Would it be agreeable to you if we were to call you Hyun-pil from now on?'

Tree-ear ducked his head quickly, recalling that the son of Min had been called Hyun-gu. A name that shared a syllable! It was an honour bestowed on siblings. No longer would Tree-ear go by the name of an orphan. He could only nod wordlessly, but he felt Ajima's smile at his back as he turned away.

'Then we will see you at suppertime, Hyun-pil,' she called softly.

Tree-ear began to jog down the path, the cart bumping before him. He had too much to think about and felt lost in the bewildering welter of his thoughts. *Crane-man . . . a wheel of my own . . . a home with Ajima, and a new name . . . Min will teach me to throw pots . . . Crane-man . . .*

Tree-ear shook his head hard, like a dog shaking off water. He groped about in his mind for an image that would calm him. A prunus vase, with a plum branch to complete its beauty—his dream of making one returned, stronger than ever now, for it would be more than a dream.

He could almost feel the clay under his hands, rising on the wheel—his own wheel!—into a shape that was grace itself. He would make replicas, dozens if need be, until the glaze was like jade and water. And the vase would be carefully, delicately inlaid, with a design of—of . . .

Tree-ear frowned a little and looked up at the mountain. The trees that were shedding the last of their leaves stood bare but dignified among the loyal green of the pines. Tree-ear's gaze followed the sweep of the trunks and branches until he saw their outlines clean and pure against the sky.

How long would it be before he had skill enough to create a design worthy of such a vase? *One hill, one valley* . . . One day at a time, he would journey through the years until he came upon the perfect design.

Tree-ear leaned forward and pushed the cart up the mountain path.

A certain prunus vase is among the most prized of Korea's many cultural treasures. It is the finest example of inlaid celadon pottery ever discovered and has been dated to the twelfth century.

The vase's most remarkable feature is its intricate inlay work. Each of the forty-six round medallions is formed by a white outer ring and a black inner ring. Within every circle, carved and then inlaid with great skill, there is a crane in graceful flight. Clouds drift between the medallions, with more cranes soaring among the clouds. And the glaze is a delicate shade of greyish green.

It is called the 'Thousand Cranes Vase'. Its maker is unknown.

AUTHOR'S NOTE

Throughout the long ages of Korean history until very recent times, few people in Korea were homeless. Both Buddhist and, later, Confucian tradition demanded that families care for relatives, even distant ones, who fell upon hard times. Those with no family were succoured by the Buddhist temples. As bridge-dwellers, Tree-ear and Crane-man would indeed have been curiosities in their time, but surely such individuals have existed in every age and society.

Korean celadon potters of the Koryo era (AD 918–1392) were initially influenced by the work of their Chinese counterparts. It is no coincidence that the two main centres for pottery, Puan—where Ch'ulp'o was located—and Kangjin, were both coastal districts with easy access to and from China across the Yellow Sea. But Korean potters were eventually to distinguish themselves in several ways: the graceful, simple shapes of their vessels; the distinctive glaze colour; the great skill of their moulded pieces; and finally, the innovation of inlay work. Every piece described in this book actually exists in a museum or private collection somewhere in the world.

Koryo celadon was renowned during its time, then ignored by the world for centuries. There was one exception: Korean celadon has always been valued in Japan. During their many invasions of the Korean peninsula, the Japanese routinely sacked royal tombs—the richest source of Koryo celadon—and spirited the treasures to Japan. Although much of this ware has been transferred back to Korean museums, the largest private collections of celadon in the world today remain in Japan. The Japanese even captured Korean potters and took them to Japan, where they were instrumental in developing the pottery industry.

Some experts speculate that the pottery trade may have been a government-run industry during the Koryo period, and that the potters in villages such as Ch'ulp'o were little more than 'factories', where labourers churned out pieces designed by appointed artists. A royal commission could have been for design rather than actual production. However, the skill of those village potters would not be lessened if this were true, and it is this I have chosen to focus on in telling a little of their story.

A law requiring potters' sons to follow the trade of their fathers is documented as having been instituted in 1543, well after the events of this story. That law appears to have had a precedent, which I have applied to Tree-ear's time, when pottery as a family trade was certainly custom, if not law.

The cause of the brown spots and impure glaze tint that ruined Min's initial work for the royal emissary is now known to be oxidation. Because it contains iron, the celadon glaze acquires the desired finish only if fired in an atmosphere of reduced oxygen. Too much air entering the kiln during the firing process will 'rust' the iron in the glaze and cause the undesirable colour. This problem was so difficult to overcome that much surviving Koryo celadon is marred by signs of oxidation. Even equipped with this knowledge and with modern electric equipment, today's potters have been unable to exactly reproduce the glorious colour achieved by past artisans.

For the account of Tree-ear's journey to Songdo, I am indebted to Simon Winchester's book *Korea: A Walk Through the Land of Miracles*. In 1987 Winchester walked the length of South Korea, from Cheju Island in the far south to Panmunjom, at the border of North Korea. Much of his trek passed through exactly the same terrain as Tree-ear's.

Readers may wonder why there is no mention of Seoul,

the current capital of Korea, which would have been directly on Tree-ear's route. Seoul was not founded until 1392, more than two hundred years after this story takes place. But Tree-ear does pass by the eventual site of the city, pausing for a look at the valley in Chapter 12.

Likewise, a modern map will not show the location of Songdo. Songdo was renamed Kaesong and is located on what is now the North Korean side of the border.

Tree-ear's seemingly irrational fear of foxes may be difficult to credit, but an analogy to bats in Western lore and literature might be helpful. Bats are really harmless creatures, yet an entire body of ghoulish bloodsucking vampire tales has grown up around them. Koreans in Tree-ear's time felt the same way about foxes, which acquired a corresponding mythos.

Tree-ear's new name was chosen in honour of Hyun-pil Chung, whose name is recorded by museums all over the world as the donor of many of the finest pieces of Korean celadon as well as other works of art. Apart from the fact that he lived in twentieth-century Korea, I have been able to learn almost nothing about this man, but because of his assiduous collecting and preservation, the public is able to view and enjoy these pieces today.

The 'Twelve Small Wonders of the World' were listed by the Chinese writer Tai-ping Lao-jen in a little-known work written during the Sung dynasty of China, contemporaneous with the Koryo era: 'The books of the Academy, the wines of the Palace, the inkstones of Tuan, the peonies of Lo-yang, the tea of Ch'ien-chou, the secret-colour ware of Koryo . . . are all first under Heaven!' The work itself is no longer extant, but several records of it exist; I came across it in Godfrey St G. M. Gompertz's *Korean Celadon*. The phrase 'radiance of jade, clarity of water' I owe to the title of the catalogue of the Ataka Collection of Korean ceramics in Osaka, Japan.

The 'Thousand Cranes Vase' can be viewed at the Kansong Museum of Art in Seoul, Korea.

Acknowledgements

I am grateful to sculptor and ceramicist Po-wen Liu, who read the manuscript of this book and offered valuable comments regarding the making of celadon ware. Any errors that remain are my responsibility.

My critique partner Marsha Hayles and my agent, Ginger Knowlton, continue to give me both enthusiastic support and critical feedback—a combination of inestimable worth to a writer. Dinah Stevenson and the people at Clarion Books have made the publication of each of my books a true pleasure.

Every story I write is for Sean and Anna. To them and to all my family, boundless gratitude—especially and always, to Ben.

© Sonya Sones

Linda Sue Park is the author of many books for young readers, including the global bestseller *A Long Walk to Water*, which has sold more than three million copies. When she is not writing, she serves on the advisory boards of We Need Diverse Books and the Society of Children's Book Writers and Illustrators. Linda Sue is also the founder of KiBooka, a listing initiative that aims to boost Korean American and Korean diasporic voices. She lives in Rochester, New York, with her family and gave a popular TED talk called *Can A Children's Book Change the World?*